THE GHOST TRAIN ARRIVED AT MIDNIGHT

Not too far in the distance, a long, drawn-out, lonesome wail sounded, the drone of an airhorn. Brian rubbed his eyes with his fists and turned on his side. But the airhorn brought him wide awake as he realized he wasn't dreaming.

He swung into a kneeling position, knocking over the telescope, and, scrambling onto his bed, he stared out the window. In the moonlight, he saw the long, dim silhouette of a train, and at its head a locomotive with a huge yellow eye, heading straight for the house.

''Mom! Dad! It's coming. It's coming fast.''

''Brian?'' He could hear his mother's drowsy voice. ''You have a nightmare?''

''The train! I saw it. The Highball Express. It's coming right at us! Hurry.''

The boy's ears were screaming with the sound of the train's whistle and horn. And then the front wall of the house exploded . . .

STEVEN SPIELBERG'S
AMAZING STORIES

STEVEN BAUER

CHARTER BOOKS, NEW YORK

STEVEN SPIELBERG'S
AMAZING STORIES

A Charter Book/published by arrangement with
MCA Publishing Rights

PRINTING HISTORY
Charter edition/October 1986

ISBN: 0-441-01906-4

Charter Books are published by The Berkley Publishing Group,
200 Madison Avenue, New York, New York 10016.
PRINTED IN THE UNITED STATES OF AMERICA

CONTENTS

The Mission   1
Vanessa in the Garden   29
Guilt Trip   49
Mr. Magic   67
The Main Attraction   91
Ghost Train   113
The Sitter   135
Santa '85   153
One for the Road   173
Hell Toupee   195
No Day at the Beach   217

THE MISSION
by Steven Bauer

Based on the Universal Television series *Amazing Stories*
Created by Steven Spielberg
Adapted from the episode ''The Mission''
Teleplay by Menno Meyjes
Story by Steven Spielberg

THE GUYS I FLEW WITH CALLED ME STATIC, STILL DO
when they write or phone, which isn't so often anymore.
Some of them are dead now, of course. But forty years
ago, in the war, I loved those guys the way a freezing
man loves a fire. They kept me alive; I needed them, and
it was mutual.

Static, see, because I manned the radio. I liked having
a nickname; I thought keeping my real name safe might
protect me if the flak was flying—but then we all had
rituals. Lamar had his crucifix and Bullseye, the bombardier, had his photograph of Betty Grable. The captain had his cigars and his pack of gum, and Jake, the
copilot, was always counting to twenty-five and holding
his breath, don't ask me why. Dave had his English/
German phrase book and his twin brother Sam was a
disciple of rabbit's feet and Norman Vincent Peale. And
all of us together, we had Jonathan, he was our lucky
piece.

We banded together in twos—Lamar and Bullseye,
Dave and Sam, Scrappy and Willy, the tail gunners, me
and Jonathan, it just happened that way. Lamar was

3

from a farm somewhere in Alabama, I think, and
Bullseye was from Michigan. They did a Yankee-Rebel
number that was pretty funny sometimes. Dave and
Sam might have been Siamese twins; they were *always*
together. I'd been the kind of kid without many friends.
I had glasses and was good in science and math. The Air
Force was the first place those talents meant anything,
the first place people liked me for who I was.

But everyone liked Jonathan, and he was my best
friend. He was an artist, real cheerful. He'd met an
English girl in Coventry and married her. They were
having a kid. After the war, he said, he was going to
California and work for Walt Disney, so I guess you
could say he had his sketch pad and his pencils and his
family to keep his mind off how close the German
ME109s came every time, spewing fire.

No one wanted to die, you see, and each time we went
up it was more than likely. *Just let me come home alive
this time,* you'd say, *and I promise this, I promise that,*
anything at all, it didn't matter, striking any bargain
that might increase your chances.

Because there was this other superstition: after
twenty-three missions, they took you out of the sky, out
of combat, let you keep your feet on solid ground.
Because no one had ever made the round trip on number
twenty-four alive.

Jonathan joined us after one flight with another crew.
So our twenty-third mission would really be his twenty-
fourth, and he wasn't flying with us. I can't tell you how
depressed we were to be going up without him.

It was January 1944, and we flew out of Coventry,
England. We called the plane the *Friendly Persuasion*

for luck, and Jonathan had painted a cartoon movie star on her nose—mesh stockings, lots of leg and cleavage, and a big inviting smile, something to come home to. It was damp and cold in the predawn darkness, and there was always fog hugging the ground, climbing to the belly of our B-17. She was battle-scarred, all right, we'd taken some fire, and her fuselage was covered with patched bullet holes. The struts and supports of the landing gear were weathered and worn, and the tires were pretty bald. But we knew her inside out, every inch, knew how to move in her. When we were flying, there were times we were almost comfortable.

As always Bullseye was supervising the loading of the bombs with the hydraulic hoist, and Lamar, inside the bomb bay, rolled them onto the racks. As always, Bullseye shouted, "Damn it, Lamar, don't stack them so close and watch it those racks ain't loose," and Lamar in his sweet low drawl said, "I'll worry about dropping 'em from six feet. You worry about dropping 'em from twenty thousand," as if this were the first time we were going up.

The rest of us slouched around, drinking coffee and slapping ourselves to keep warm. Jake was counting to twenty-five, and Sam was reading *The Power of Positive Thinking*. Me? I was just scared to death.

The captain walked up to the plane, his sheepskin collar turned against the damp. He looked great, unruffled as the leather of his jacket, and he had an unlit cigar clamped between his teeth. Nothing seemed to shake him. "Up and at 'em, boys," he said.

The ground crew had just finished fueling up the *Friendly Persuasion*, but none of us jumped to our feet.

I looked around for my buddy, but there wasn't anybody there but us.

"How are we going to fly without Jonathan?" I said.

"You said he was going to be here for our lucky rub," Bullseye said.

The captain grinned as though his face hurt. I knew he didn't like going up without Jonathan any more than the rest of us, but he wasn't going to show it. "I was just telling the old man, Colonel, you can say a lot of things about my crew, but you can't say they're superstitious," he said.

"You want to go up with a green belly-gunner?" Sam asked.

The captain shrugged. Then I saw the jeep.

"Hey, look!" I said. It was moving fast down the tarmac toward us, its lights swinging crazily in the dark.

"Probably the new kid," Jake said, the cynic.

But it wasn't; it was Jonathan, good as his word, coming to let us rub his head for luck. He was smiling and bleary-eyed, and he jumped out of the jeep wearing his flight gear. Boy, it was good to see him.

"What do you say, Static?" He punched me on the shoulder. "Morning, fellas."

"You're supposed to be in civvies," I said.

"They're okay for the soda fountain," he said, "but a little on the thin side for Berlin in January."

Everyone was crowding around us, smiling now, feeling better. But the captain didn't smile. "Jonathan," he said. "Can I have a word with you?" They walked away until the captain thought they were out of earshot, but I moved close enough to hear.

"You don't have to do this, you know," the captain said.

Jonathan was cracking gum. "We've flown twenty-two missions together and well, *hell,* sir, I'm your lucky charm. You wouldn't fly without insurance, would you?"

Another jeep pulled in, and a guy stood up in a hurry, smacking his head on the underside of the wing. He winced, bent over, and fell from the jeep. Jonathan's replacement. Under other circumstances, it would have been funny. We all looked away.

"Well, Captain," Jonathan said. "What you see before you is an actual dilemma. You gonna fly your last mission with a green gunner or a jinxed one?"

I swallowed hard. The captain shifted from hip to hip. You could almost see him weighing the alternatives. Then he grinned and reached up and yanked off Jonathan's leather flak cap and rubbed his hair. We all cheered, crowding around them, almost poking his eyes out as we each rubbed Jonathan's head.

The way out was always tense. We did our jobs and talked and fooled around. The captain and Jake were in the cockpit, flying the plane. I plotted the course. The gunners sat against the fuselage getting nervous. In a little while they'd clean and load their guns. Jonathan usually drew. He sat near me while I checked the maps.

"So how much longer before we can call you dad?" I asked.

He was concentrating, and his tongue bothered the side of his mouth. "About four months," he said, "but Liz has never been on time for anything in her life so I'm not holding my breath. She thought that if it's a boy, we'd give him your real name."

I was flattered, of course. But I'd never told any of

the guys; only the captain knew. "You really want a kid," I said, "called Arnold?"

He looked at me for a minute the way the guys in high school used to. "*Arnold*," he said. "For real?" If it was now, of course, I would have said, "Like Schwarzenegger." But back then it was a name for dorks. "Yeah," I said. "Like Benedict Arnold."

"Not you, buddy," he said. "You're true blue."

I wanted to change the subject. "You're going to take her stateside, aren't you?"

"Sure," he said. "She's a citizen now." Then he thought about me and my plans. "Hey, did you hear? Did you get accepted?"

"I didn't tell you? Minnesota U. Twin City engineering department, GI bill. We'll have to stay in touch, bud."

"We'll do better than that. You'll come to California and watch me work my way up from the paint and ink department to Mickey himself."

"Will you introduce me to Rita Hayworth?"

"How about Mr. Disney?" Jonathan said. "I should be calling him Walt by then."

"Places," the captain said, and Jon shrugged and got to his feet, making his way back to the belly turret, this little swiveling Plexiglas bubble under the plane where he hung unprotected and alone. I hated to see him go, always did. "See you," I said. He grinned and winked at me and went down.

Then the gum came back. Each trip the captain opened a big pack of Wrigley's and we all took a piece, passing it through the plane like communion or something. I got up and handed it back to Sam.

"We're gonna buy the farm on this trip," he was saying to his brother. "I can feel it. I can smell it. I got it in my mouth like some foul taste."

"Oh, shut up," Dave said. "You know when I start to worry? The time you *don't* say that."

Sam stuck a piece through the hatch of the belly turret, and Jonathan took it. I didn't know how he could stand it down there. It was cramped and real cold, with nothing between you and the ground below but plastic and aluminum struts. He didn't seem to mind, though. I saw his hand shoot up, holding a piece of paper, and Dave grabbed it.

"Hey, can I see?" Sam said.

"It's not for you," Dave said and snuck a peek, then handed it to me. I handed it on to Bullseye and Lamar, and it made its way to the cockpit. It was a cartoon of the *Friendly Persuasion* with two eyes and a mouth, and all our heads sticking out windows, everyone, even the plane, looking spooked. *Lucky 24, who's smiling now?* it said. He'd drawn one like it every time we'd gone up, and the cockpit was plastered with the other twenty-two. But this time the number was Jonathan's number, not the plane's, and it seemed a little weird.

I gave the captain the weather update over the radio, and then I saw Jonathan's parachute stuck against the side with a sketch pad under its straps. I couldn't resist.

Lamar came over, fingering his crucifix.

"What are you doing after today?" I said.

He turned his palms to the ceiling. "Suppose I'll be instructin' a gang of gung-ho rowdies same as we all used to be."

"Take a look at these," I said.

"Maybe we wasn't supposed to find them," he said.

"You know Jonathan, always lookin' to surprise us one way or other."

They were cartoons of us. Jake sat before a massive control panel, his eight blurred arms pulling levers and pressing buttons. The captain was posing as War Hero, bent slightly under the weight of his medals, his hat too big for his head. Lamar was seated backwards on a cow. Scrappy was riding what looked like a big chicken.

"That a chicken or a turkey he's on?" Lamar said.

"Maybe it's a duck," I said. "There's you, farm boy."

"Yeah," Lamar said, almost reverently. "There's you."

I had headphones on, like powderpuffs, and huge glasses and electrified hair. "Here's to all of us," I said.

"Class of '44," Lamar said.

Sam and Dave were kneeling by their fifty-calibers, cleaning and loading. I was going to show them their pictures, the two of them heavy with rabbit's feet and books and all of their fingers crossed, but they were too busy torturing each other.

"We been real lucky," Dave said, as if to himself.

Sam blanched. "Swallow it," he said.

"Twenty-two outings, twenty-two homecomings," Dave said.

"Ixnay!" Sam said. "You'll jinx the last round trip."

Dave took out his phrase book and gave Sam a piece of something. "Look what I picked up in Coventry," he said. "Lieutenant's bars. If we gotta bail, put 'em on your collar. Then say, 'Ich bin ein Amerikanischer Offizier.' "

Sam grabbed the phrase book away and dug in his jacket. He pulled out *The Power of Positive Thinking*.

"Read some more of this," he said, thrusting it at his brother, "and don't talk to me again until we land."

Instead, I showed the cartoons to Scrappy, the tail gunner, who was chewing his nails. "Why can't *I* do that?" he said. He shook his head.

"Jonathan's got all the imagination," I said.

"I got six ME109s," Scrappy said. "What's that make me?"

"A hero," I said. "After the war that and a nickel will get you a cup of coffee. But Jonathan, he's got the old imagination. We'll all be working for him some day."

That's when we got hit.

The *Friendly Persuasion* jolted upwards and to the left. I could smell the cordite. Everyone was yelling and scrambling into position. After all these trips, I thought. We'd taken fire before, but this was worse. Wind whistled through the fuselage. The voices of other pilots came cracking over the radio.

"Bandits at eleven o'clock."

"Bandits at six o'clock."

"Watch your wing. He's on your tail, Jack."

And then the worst. "We're hit. I'm burning." Then nothing.

Behind me Dave and Sam were blasting for their lives, knees slightly bent, swiveling, firing into the white air. I wondered how Jonathan was, under us all. He'd be twisting like a top right now, trying to track the bastards, watching as they suddenly pierced the cloud cover and were right on top of him, spitting fire; he'd be firing back, his whole body rattling under the spasms of the .50 twin Brownings.

We got hit again, bad. I could hear the whine and whistle of incoming ammo, and the stutter of our guns in return. We were really in it. Dave staggered backwards and hit Sam's oxygen bottle. The radio had turned to squawks and garbled noise. Right below and behind us in the air, there was a terrific explosion. "Whoopee!" Scrappy yelled. "I think Jonathan got hisself one." And then another explosion as part of the German plane collided with ours; flaming metal blasted into our B-17 and a fuel tank exploded, almost tearing a wing off. It was crazy. Everyone was falling down and screaming; Lamar was saying Hail Marys faster than I'd ever heard him talk before. The lights went out. Along the plane's ribs, electric wires sparked and hissed. I closed my eyes and thought of my parents. I was only nineteen.

Then the captain's voice came over the intercom. "Salvo 'em, Bullseye."

"Yessir," Bullseye said and pulled two levers downward. The bomb bay doors opened and the bombs rolled off the rails, disappearing into the blanket of clouds beneath us. The *Friendly Persuasion* responded right away, gaining altitude after the loss of the bombs, buoyant again. For the first time since we'd been hit, I thought we might make it.

"I want damage reports from all stations," the captain said over the intercom. "Tail gunner."

"Okay back here, sir," Scrappy said into his throat mike.

"Door gunners."

"Bad dents and a rip, but okay, sir," Sam said, and then Dave.

"Belly gunner."

There was no reply.

"Captain to belly gunner. Report," the captain said. "Come on, Jonathan," the captain said, his voice rising. "What the devil is going on?"

And then Jonathan's voice, shaky but there. "It must of been the concussion, sir," he said. "That lousy mosquito gave me a bloody nose. The plexi's all spider-webbed and crazy."

"But you're okay?" the captain asked.

"Yeah," Jonathan said. "I'm okay."

"You swatted him but good, kid. Get topside and let one of the men take a look at you."

After a minute Jonathan's voice came over the intercom, a little puzzled and scared. "Captain, I'm having some trouble getting the hatch open."

"Jonathan's having trouble with his hatch. Somebody give him a hand," the captain said. But it wasn't necessary. We were already there, me and Dave and Sam. The piece of ME109 which had hit us had landed on part of the turret's hatch, welding it shut. We pulled on the goddamn thing, but it wouldn't budge. I could see Jonathan down there, trying to smile. The bottom part of his face was covered with blood. "Did I ever tell you guys I got this fear of small places?" he shouted above the plane's roar.

Dave cupped his mouth and yelled down into the turret. "You're stuck in mama's belly till we can land and torch you out."

"I don't think I'll bleed to death," Jon said. "Okay, Dave, sure. Don't worry about me."

"My God, will you look at that," Sam said and pointed out under the wings.

Over the intercom, the captain said, "We're taking

her home, boys. Number twenty-three over and out. We're going home. Static, bring the fact sheets on up here."

I grabbed my clipboard from the hook by the radio and stumbled up to the cockpit. "Let's have it, Static," the captain said.

"We burnt seventeen hundred gallons en route to primary target, sir," I said. "We lost one hundred when number three outboard blew. We can make it back to Coventry if the winds are good to us. But I gotta believe the underside of this baby is torn to pieces."

"She's flying heavy to the right. I can feel it," Jake said.

"I was wondering, sir," I said. "Well, I was wondering if you'd tried the landing gear." I could feel my heart pounding in my throat.

The captain looked at me strangely, then flipped the switch. The three of us watched as nothing happened, no whining sound of the wheels lowering, no light on the control panel.

"Bullseye," the captain said, "take a look and tell me if you see any wheel in the down and lock position." The silence lasted just a few seconds while he peered out the bombardier's window.

"It's a junkyard under both wings," Bullseye said. "You'll have to toboggan us in."

The captain took a cigar from his pocket and clenched it in his teeth. "I never landed wheels up before, but hell, we'll be bone dry by that time and the only thing on fire will be this cigar."

I could see he didn't have all the facts yet, and I knew I had to be the one to tell him. "We got a problem, sir," I said. "A real problem." My voice got shaky, like I was going to cry. "It's Jonathan, sir. He's trapped in the belly turret and we can't get him out."

The captain closed his eyes and his leather gloves clenched the steering. "We're going belly in with thirty tons of airplane on a concrete runway?" he said. "I don't really think eleven hundred pounds of plexi and aluminum will hold up under all that weight. Do you?" He unstrapped himself, told Jake to hold steady, and stepped back into the fuselage to tend to the problem himself.

He was a good man, the captain, but he wasn't a blowtorch, and that's the only thing that could have helped. He kicked at the welded metal and swore; he grabbed a crowbar-type thing and pried and banged away, but nothing happened. We all of us tugged and pulled and kicked, but the only thing we did was bend the bastard a little. And then Jon's hand stuck up through the opening, cool as you please. It held another cartoon, the *Friendly Persuasion* coming in for a landing with Jonathan's legs stuck out to stop it, wearing these big rubber boots. *Whoaa* it read in a cartoon balloon.

"You mean he knows?" Dave said. "He knows?"

"I guess he got the picture," I said, and it wasn't a joke.

The captain waved us back and knelt down so he could talk to Jonathan. "How you doing in there, kid?" he asked.

I could barely hear the reply. "I'm scared, Captain," Jon said. "But I know you'll work something out. You won't let anything happen to me 'cause I'm your lucky charm, right?"

The captain's voice was soft. "We're in a real pickle, kid," he said. "But I guess you know that already."

"I'm not going to die in here," Jon said. "I got too much to live for."

"Jonathan, listen," the captain said.

"Just rub my head for good luck, sir," Jon said. "I know you'll think of something. You always do."

The captain leaned over so his whole arm was missing from view. "Sure, kid," he said. "I'll think of something."

Jake's voice came over the intercom. "Captain, we're losing number four outboard." I was connected to the cockpit by radio now, and had just called Coventry and put them on alert. "I told the tower we'll be landing wheels up, time approximate, twelve minutes."

"Crack the cowl flaps on number two," the captain said.

"Number two cracked," Jake said.

"Close fuel shut-off valve."

"Fuel shut-off closed."

"Set number two fire extinguisher."

"Set."

The crew had been conferring, brainstorming, and now they went past me to talk to the captain. I wasn't going to miss out on a chance to help Jonathan; if I needed to, I could get back to the radio in seconds. "It's like this, sir," Lamar said. "We been rackin' our brains."

"We got a couple of crazy ideas, Captain," Sam said.

"Like hanging one of those fifty-calibers from a rope, see, then lowering it out the left waist door," Dave said.

"Then you angle the nose down like this, see," Lamar said, "and maybe that rope drifts by Jonathan's plexi. He kicks through and hangs on and we reel him in like an old lake bass."

"We're down to fifteen hundred horsepower, boys," the captain said. "We got all but two engines left. Hear what I'm saying? This plane's built to do a lot of tricks, but not on crutches. I got another idea. Static, hand me my chute."

I grabbed it from the back of his chair, where he couldn't reach it.

"We already thought of that, Captain," Bullseye said. "The chute won't fit through that hole back there."

"Not like this, it won't," the captain said. "Take it out of the pack and roll it tight as you can. Jake, what's the minimum bailout altitude?"

"Fifteen hundred feet, sir."

"It's been done from twelve hundred," I said. I knew. I'd seen men do it.

"Get back there," the captain said. "We haven't got a spare second. I'll tell Jonathan."

We ran for it all right, Bullseye pulling the chute from its casing as fast as he could. We heard the captain's voice over the intercom. "Jonathan," he said. "I thought of something."

We'd rolled it tight and begun feeding it down into the belly turret. Jonathan's face was white as the thin silk, and the blood on his chin was caked and flaking. "Now as soon as you get that chute," the captain said, "I want you to kick out the plexi, hold that baby tight to your chest and jump away from the propwash. You hear that? Jump *away*. It'd look really bad to come in with a bloody tail."

We were pushing as fast as we could, feeding it down.

"Call out some altitudes," Bullseye said into his throat mike.

"Two thousand feet," Jake said.

I could feel the tension on the chute as Jonathan tugged. "Relax," I yelled to him. "Take it easy."

"Slow down, boy," Lamar said, trying to be reassuring. "We only got one shot at this."

"Sixteen hundred feet," Jake said.

"Faster," Jonathan said. "I don't know how long it'll take to get the plexi out. Maybe I should start kicking now."

"Captain says wait until you got the harness on," I said.

"Come on, come on, come on," Jon said. I'd never seen him ruffled before.

"Fifteen hundred feet," Jake said.

"Can't he hold us steady a couple more seconds?" Sam said.

"He ain't got the fuel," Lamar said. "As it is, we're coasting on a prayer the last bit."

"Thirteen hundred feet," Jake said.

"Let's *go*," Jonathan said. He was panicking. He tugged as hard as he could, and the edge we'd been worrying got away and snagged on the jagged edge of the hole. I've heard silk rip once since then, when my wife caught a scarf on a nail, and I damn near passed out. It's like an otherworldly screaming, magnified by reverb, the sound of the bottom falling out. Jon kept pulling and pulling, tearing the chute, like a reflex action. I looked at Lamar and there were tears in his eyes.

"I ripped the chute, Captain," Jon said, his voice low and cautious, as though he had finally understood he might really die. "It's my fault. Come on, let's have another chute."

But we were too low, I knew. We'd have to climb again, and if we did, we'd run out of fuel and all of us would die. At that moment, it hardly seemed to matter. I decided to try. I ran to the cockpit and grabbed the back of the captain's chair.

"Just another hundred feet, sir," I said, "and hold that for a couple minutes."

"You know math, and you know the landscape," he said, turning to me. "What's the point just before the field?"

"Just the forest," I said. I saw us smashing into the trunks of trees, exploding in a fireball. I saw us gliding over their crowns, and Jon bailing out, impaling himself on a branch.

Jon's voice came over the intercom. "Belly gunner to pilot," he said. "Can you hear me, sir? Any ideas yet? I can see Manchester woods; we should be pretty close to home now."

I turned around and stumbled back toward the others, the tears hot on my cheeks, not even embarrassed. Lamar was crying too.

Over the intercom, the parry and thrust of the captain's voice and Jake's sounded deadly, inhuman.

"Set altimeter, two niner niner two."

"Two niner niner two check."

"Booster pumps?"

"On."

"Intercoolers?"

"Aren't you going to answer him?" Jake asked.

The captain exploded. "What the hell you want me to say? Thanks for the insurance? We're all gonna make it, but your policy's up? Intercoolers!''

"Intercoolers. Cold.''

"Cowl flaps.''

"Cowl flaps opened and locked,'' Jake said.

"Auto mixture rich,'' the captain said.

Inside the belly turret Jonathan was yelling. "I had a good life before the war and all during it too. I got to see Europe from the air. I got me a wife. I flew twenty-three missions without a scratch. So don't you guys worry. I'm gonna survive this one. Bet on it. You know how we can see our own deaths? Well, I know I'm not supposed to die this way.''

The tower was calling us in now. I'd told them the story, and they had fire equipment standing by. They'd gone and gotten a priest, goddamn them, and wanted me to hook him up to the intercom. At first I refused, but the commander himself got on and said, real cool, "That's an order, Sergeant.''

A voice came over the line, reedy and slow as honey in a cold kitchen. "Jonathan, I'm Father McKay. Is there anything I can do for you, son?''

I hated the bastard. Jonathan didn't need this, last rites, before it was even over. He'd think of something; the captain would think of something. Besides, Jon wasn't even Catholic.

He talked right back. "I'm not going to die, Father. There's other guys worse off who could use your prayers. My number's not up. I don't know how I know this, but I do. Captain's gonna think of something before it's too late.''

But if Jonathan and I hadn't given up, the others had. They queued to give his head a final lucky rub. They knelt and reached down and he called them each by name and let them touch his head—inside, the cartoons must have been forming and dissolving like snow on water—the head which would split like a melon when the airplane dropped its weight on him, crushing him between fuselage and runway. We'd seen death before, and had all lost friends, but this was the worst by far, like seeing not so much your own death as the death of all possibility. It was worse than if the plane with all of us in it was going down.

When it was my turn, I knelt and reached my hand in and scratched my wrist on the metal. The scrape felt good. I couldn't look at him.

"Static," he said. "I want you to take Liz to the States with you. I want my baby to be born in California." I didn't say a word, something I've always regretted. I could feel him gripping my hand with both of his, and then he kissed it. I pulled my hand back as though it had been scalded and huddled with the others away from the hatch.

Lamar had taken his crucifix off the gold chain on which he usually wore it. Bullseye's picture of Betty Grable, wrinkled and torn, was clutched in his meaty hands. Dave's lieutenant bars didn't look like they were helping him much as he watched his brother stroke a rabbit's foot like it was Aladdin's lamp.

"It ain't gonna be quick, you know," Lamar said.

"Stow it," Dave said. "Just shut up."

But Lamar wasn't finished. "You think one of us should . . . I mean if it was me, I know I'd want one of you to . . . Bullseye? You're my buddy, you'd do it for me, wouldn't ya? Static? You're his best friend, ain't you?"

I looked down at the .45 in my shoulder holster; it

was regulation issue, supposed to give you a bit more confidence if you had to bail out behind enemy lines. I hadn't shot it since target practice during training, the same week they taught us to jump and tuck and fall like a bomb through the air until it was time to pull the chute cord, but I'd cleaned it religiously, and its clip was ready for action. Its grip was hard, cold, black when I touched it.

Voices were coming over the radio now, which I'd hooked up to the intercom. The captain to us and to Jake, the tower signaling numbers, the chaplain or priest or whoever he was—all of them talking, sometimes at once, as though the world was ending and the decent pauses between conversation had been wiped out because there wasn't any time left.

"I want everyone to assume crash positions," the captain said. "When we go down to the ground, I'll ring the alarm and then everybody get the hell out and away from this bird."

"Then I saw new heavens and a new earth." I thought of my buddy coming in for a landing on his back; I could imagine how I'd feel—the sweat in my armpits, on my chest with nowhere to go until I was bathed in it, the tears my eyes would be squeezing out, the way I'd have made half-moons in my palms with my fingernails, the pressure in my jaw as I crushed my teeth together—and I thought it might not be too bad to go quickly. *"The former heavens and the former earth had passed away and the sea was no longer,"* the priest intoned.

In the cockpit, I guessed the captain was chewing a cigar and Jake was counting to twenty-five, the numbers a blur as he whizzed through and started at zero. The

Power of Positive Thinking. I tried to imagine a safe landing, but my mind kept hitting the hard cement facts. I took the gun from my shoulder holster.

"Carburetor filters," the captain said, as if it were part of the litany.

"Filters on," Jake, the congregation, intoned.

"Hydraulic pressure."

"Seven hundred pounds."

The Lord be with you.

And with your spirit . . .

"Turbos."

"Turbos set. Steady on course. Twelve hundred feet, one one thousand, one thousand feet."

"Wind zero six six zero to two zero to three zero," the tower said.

"Nine hundred feet," Jake said. "Speed one sixty, eight hundred feet."

"I also saw a new Jerusalem, the holy city coming out of heaven from God, beautiful as a bride prepared to meet her husband." I thought of Liz, and remembered she *always* was there to meet our plane; whether we got back early or late, she kept a vigil at the airfield. Was she down there now, watching us come in with her husband hanging underneath the plane?

I took the .45 from my holster and loaded the clip. We were low now, very close. I could almost sense the ground whizzing below us. The engines started to sputter; we were out of fuel.

"Wind oh-nine-oh at thirty to thirty-five," the tower said.

"Seven hundred feet," Jake said.

"Help me out here," the captain said. "More left rudder."

"Five hundred, correcting for drift," Jake said.

"Wing flaps one-third."

"One-third."

"More RPMs?"

"Twenty-two hundred," Jake said.

"Bump it again," the captain commanded.

The gun was heavy. *"I heard a loud voice from the throne ring out this is God's dwelling among men. He shall dwell with them and they shall be his people and he shall be their God who is always with them."*

I inched toward the belly turret until I could just glimpse the top of Jonathan's head; he'd taken his cap off so everyone could rub his hair, and it was mussed and curly and dark with sweat. I cocked the gun and looked back at Lamar and Bullseye, Dave and Sam. Only Lamar was looking at me, approval in his eyes. Just another inch; I could see Jonathan writing on his pad in a frenzy, maybe a note to Liz. I'd take her back with me; I'd stay with her in California. The hell with engineering.

"Five hundred feet, four-fifty," Jake said.

"Lifting the nose," the captain said. "Wing flaps fully extended. High RPMs."

"Full flaps. Number two oil temp up in the red."

"Too late to worry about that now," the captain said.

"He shall wipe every tear from their eyes."

And then Jonathan's voice came over the intercom, clear and confident. "Captain," he said. "Try it one more time. Try it once for me."

"And there shall be no more death or mourning, crying out or pain, for the former world has passed away."

"One hundred feet, Captain," Jake said. "Seventy-five. Sixty feet. Throttling back."

Benedict Arnold, I thought. The gun was shaking in my hand. I felt the pressure of the trigger on my finger. I closed my eyes tight. "I can't do it," I whispered. "I can't do it." I pulled back the gun from my friend's head.

"Holy shit," Bullseye said. His voice was high and thin, drenched in awe. "Will you look at that?" he said. He was staring out the Plexiglas of the bombardier's nose cone, as he had when the captain asked him to report on the status of the landing gear. He backed away and crossed himself, and I pushed forward and crowded in.

Even now I find it hard to believe, even though it happened to me, but I was there, and I'm telling you God's honest truth. Where the wheels should have been were these huge rubber tires, yellow as a daffodil, yellow as forsythia, the kind of yellow you only see in cartoons, attached to the plane by these thin metal legs, striped white and red like a barber pole.

Just then we touched ground, we could feel the solidity of earth beneath us, but it was the smoothest landing we'd ever made, like we'd landed on a foam pillow, like the earth itself was made of rubber. We cheered and cheered, tears streaming down our faces; we ripped off our flak caps and hugged each other. We were yelling like we'd never yelled before. We were safe.

"Captain, I'm seeing things," Bullseye said into his throat mike. "The gear's down, but I'm still seeing things. 'Cause it's, well, it's . . ."

"It's a miracle," the captain said.

"You don't know the half of it," Bullseye said.

We jumped from the plane, fast as we could, and the rest of the crew, who hadn't seen what Bullseye and I knew, stopped short in their tracks. Sam fell to his knees; Lamar put the crucifix *in his mouth*. Dave walked forward as if hypnotized, his hands outstretched toward the cartoon wheels. He almost touched one, but it moved toward him, it bulged out to meet his fingers; it opened and squirted a bright shower of sparks, like gold dust, into the air.

I stared at Jonathan in the belly turret. He was asleep, or in a dream, or something. His eyes were closed and his lips were wreathed in the most peaceful smile I've ever seen. Lamar came over and started banging on the plexi, but the captain grabbed him by the jacket and pulled him back.

"Don't touch him," he said. "Let's get a torch over here on the double. Cut him out of there. Do it! Don't wake him up. Don't jostle him one inch."

It only took a minute. The blue flame of the acetylene torch showered the runway with yellow sparks, and we cut out a hole just big enough to slide Jonathan out, clutching his sketch pad to his chest. Then we carried him like a wounded soldier off the tarmac and into the waist-high grass of the field nearby and gently set him down.

I looked back at the airplane. The *Friendly Persuasion* stood there, safe after its twenty-third mission, ripped by shrapnel and bullets, and impossibly held up by these huge yellow wheels, like gigantic inner tubes, like *doughnuts*. They shimmered, even in broad daylight; their edges danced and raced as if they were alive.

"Jonathan!" the captain yelled. "Can you hear me? Wake up, kid. Snap out of it. Come on, boy. Snap out of it!" He slapped Jon across the face, pretty hard, and he twitched; his eyes flickered once and then opened.

Behind us, we heard the sound of tearing metal. I whirled around in time to see the barber poles and yellow wheels flicker and disappear, and the body of the B-17 smashed to the runway with a huge crash. The belly turret shattered, and aluminum struts and pieces of Plexiglas flew in the air.

"What happened?" Jonathan stammered. "Did we make it?"

I looked down at Jon lying there. His face was still white, and dried blood still covered his lips and chin. Across the tarmac, I could see Liz running toward us. On the sketch pad on his chest was a cartoon of the *Friendly Persuasion*, its fuselage torn and battered, its props stuttering. And where the landing gear should have been these skinny striped poles stuck out and ended in huge, patched, bulbous yellow wheels, like doughnuts.

"How in God's name did he do that?" I said.

"Hey," Jake said. "He's got all the luck."

"He's got all the talent," Bullseye said.

"He's got all the imagination," Sam said. "All the goddamn imag*in*ation."

And then, one by one, starting with the captain, we all, each one of us, reached down and rubbed Jonathan's hair.

VANESSA
IN THE GARDEN
by Steven Bauer

Based on the Universal Television series *Amazing Stories*
Created by Steven Spielberg
Adapted from the episode ''Vanessa in the Garden''
Teleplay by Steven Spielberg

"I CAN'T STAND STILL A MOMENT LONGER," VANESSA said. "I have an itch."

The tip of the brush, brilliant with cadmium red, paused before the canvas, and Byron Sullivan shifted his attention to his wife as she stood motionless and elegant against the backdrop of their country garden. It was the height of summer in New Hampshire and the long-stemmed roses, red and yellow, surrounded Vanessa as if she were a princess among a host of attendants. As always, he was astonished by her beauty; at eighteen, she seemed poised to break into otherworldliness. Her blonde hair was piled high on her head, coiffed in the current late nineteenth-century fashion so becoming to her. The soft blush her posing had brought to her cheeks seemed a faint mirror of the roses against the white lace of her ribbon-bedecked dress. The shadow of her parasol fell neatly at her feet, a small puddle of dark ground.

"Then I suggest you scratch it," he said.

31

"I can't reach it. It's in the small of my back."

"Try not to think of it," he said, looking at the canvas.

"I can't *not* think about it," Vanessa said.

"Then think of something else," he said. "I'm very nearly done."

"Tell me what to think of," Vanessa said. "Or I'll go mad."

He needed her to stay still another ten minutes. The light he'd almost captured would never be the same. The canvas, splashed with sun, gay with the reds and yellows of the roses, was one of the best he'd ever done, luminous and mysterious. He'd captured, somehow—even he could see—not Vanessa herself, but her essence and the spirit of the roses. He was sure, in December, that the canvas would flood any room in which it hung with the sweet, heady smell of summer. But more than that, he knew: anyone seeing the painting would be gladdened, would know that this was painted not so much with pigments as with love. He kept painting, trying to distract her from the itch.

"Where were you, oh, say, one year ago this minute?"

Vanessa's expression changed from slightly pained composure to amusement. "You know very well exactly where I was," she said. "I was with you."

"Ah yes," he said. Just a few minutes more. The parasol needed shading; he hadn't gotten the light exactly right. "I do seem to remember."

"*Seem* to remember!"

"Nothing too specific," he said. "A vague recollection." He looked at her and smiled. "Only each and every glorious moment."

She seemed to have forgotten all about her itch. "Tell me," she said.

Byron felt as though the white paint floated from his brush to the parasol's ribs, and he could see he'd caught the brightness of the sun without its harshness. "I see you in the early morning with the fishermen on the banks of the Seine. I see you standing under the Arc de Triomphe during the sun shower. And I see you reading in the Tuileries while children play around you." He'd moved to the folds of her dress now, to the lace's eyelets and the shadows they threw.

"What was I reading?" she asked.

"*That* I don't remember."

"And why not?" Vanessa said. He was afraid for a moment that her face might assume the pout of her voice, but she continued looking serenely at him as though this standing still weren't torture.

"Because, my dear Vanessa, all I really remember of Paris is you. Not the books, not the plays, not even the paintings. Only you."

Vanessa smiled, and it was as if the sun had just begun shining. He stood back and critically examined his canvas: it was rough around the edges, surely, but he'd caught that moment, the play of sun and shadow, the colors singing to each other, as if the painting had a voice and it was Vanessa's. "You may scratch," he said. "I can finish the rest without your rapt attention. Come look."

She dropped the parasol to the ground, where it rolled among the roses. Then, in the first ungraceful move she'd made that day, she reached behind her and tried to rub her back. "Come here," he said. "I'll scratch it for you."

She stood beside him. She carried with her the odor of roses, the gold coins of strewn sunlight. He ran the fingers of his hand up and down her spine as she studied the painting. He could feel the intake of her breath. "What's the matter?" he asked. "You don't like it?"

Vanessa turned to him and threw her arms around him. "Oh, Byron," she said. "It's exquisite. Am I that lovely?"

"I haven't done you justice," Byron said, and meant it.

Byron always enjoyed visiting Teddy Shearing and his wife Eve. Though they were of an earlier generation—Teddy had been born before the Civil War—he felt as though he'd known them all his life, and since Teddy had become his dealer and agent, their friendship, far from waning and becoming a professional relationship, had blossomed. Teddy was, well, like a father to him, and here in New Hampshire, where the society of younger people was sparse indeed, his closest confidant. As he approached the Shearings', he could hear the sounds of a game in progress; rounding the corner, he saw Teddy and Eve playing badminton with a couple he didn't recognize. All in white, the four volleyed and shouted good-naturedly; Byron watched as Teddy charged the net and with an overhand slam landed the shuttlecock just within the back boundary.

"Well done, Teddy, well done," Byron said, and it was only then the foursome noticed him.

"Byron!" Teddy said. "Wonderful to see you."

"Not bad for an old rapscallion," Byron said. Then Eve was beside him and he took her hand and kissed it. "Eve, you look lovely, as always," he said.

Eve blushed, something she was good at. "Byron," she said. "You're charming, as always."

The other couple stood before them now and Eve moved aside. "Dr. and Mrs. Edward Northrope, may I introduce our good friend Byron Sullivan."

"The young Impressionist Teddy's told us so much about? He says you're brilliant," Mrs. Northrope said.

"He's my agent," Byron said.

"When will we have an opportunity to see your work, young man?" Dr. Northrope asked. He wore gold-rimmed spectacles; behind them his eyes glittered like mica.

"I . . . I think it best if Teddy answer that."

"In due time," Teddy said.

There was a pause that began to get uncomfortable, but Eve rescued them all. "I've worked up quite an appetite," she said. "Anyone care for lunch, or should I eat it all myself?"

"I believe I could force down a bite," Dr. Northrope said.

"Then why don't we adjourn to the main house? Byron, do join us."

"I'd love to," Byron said.

"We'll be with you in a moment, dear," Teddy said. "I'd like a private word with Byron."

"Don't be too long, Teddy," Eve said, "or I can't promise there'll be anything left to eat."

Byron winked at her, which made her blush again and smile, and he shook both the Northropes' hands before the three of them turned and walked away across the emerald lawn. Teddy took Byron's arm as if they were classmates at Oxford, and the two strolled over toward an intricate gazebo the Shearings had had built under a stately old chestnut. Teddy had news for him, Byron could tell; he always appeared nonchalant and blasé when he was busy trying not to look excited.

"And how is your lovely Vanessa?" he murmured distractedly, his eyes sweeping the branches of the tree as if searching for the green horned cases of the chestnuts.

"Very well, thank you," Byron said. "I can't tell you how happy she makes me."

"I know, I know," Teddy said. "Marvelous being your age, in such strong health, at the height of your powers. I've never seen you in better spirits or more productive in your work."

Byron could stand it no longer. "I was told you had to see me," he said.

"I have something for you." Teddy pulled out an envelope and handed it to Byron.

"What's this?"

"Can't you read?"

"*Theodore Shearing cordially invites you to a presentation of new works by Byron Sullivan, on August 17th at The Colman Gallery, New York, New York.*"

"You're ready for a major show, my boy. Congratulations."

"But Teddy, The Colman Gallery? Whistler has exhibited there. And Sargent, and Cassatt . . . "

"And soon Byron Sullivan, a major new talent. I have advances for half your work already. I'm sorry to say you're going to be very wealthy and famous and admired."

Byron's ears were hot, and he could feel himself beginning to tremble. "I've got to tell Vanessa," he said. He whooped, hugged Teddy, and leapt off the gazebo's platform, nearly slipping in his haste and excitement.

"Careful, Byron," Teddy said. "Let's try to stay alive."

As he ran across the lawn, he yelled over his shoulder, "Give my regrets to Eve. I'm sorry."

He heard Teddy's faint voice floating after him. "Quite all right. We understand." He knew they did; he knew they understood about Vanessa.

Later, even after the initial shock and horror had worn off, Byron had some trouble reconstructing the rest of that day. He'd run breathless to his horse and galloped home to discover Vanessa at the piano playing Brahms. She seemed almost unreal to him as his good fortune doubled and tripled before him—having the freedom and space to apply his talent, having Teddy as an agent, most of all having Vanessa as his muse, his lover, his wife. He wouldn't tell her right away; instead, he made elaborate excuses, ridiculous explanations. He hired a carriage, and though the night was rain- and wind-swept, they went off to the Derby Inn for pheasant stuffed with quail eggs and wild rice, and a bottle of the finest French champagne. And then, with the candles guttering around them, he told her. He could remember, and always would, how large her eyes had become, how she'd covered her mouth with her gloved hand, how she'd said, "Now the whole world will know what I know."

They'd been totally giddy, slightly drunk on the way home, and the sound of their singing almost drowned out the rain and the harsh oaths of the carriage driver. But it had no effect upon the sudden jolt he felt when the horse shied away from a fallen tree and the wooden wheels slithered sideways in the mud and the carriage toppled sideways down a ravine. That's when things got especially fuzzy. He remembered blood on his starched shirt, but was it his or hers? And that gash of cadmium red across his wife's untroubled forehead? When had the singing turned to screams?

At her funeral, everyone was kind, or so he was told. He didn't listen to the mourners streaming past him, speaking useless words of comfort, asking if there were any way to help; he ate nothing of the meal Teddy and Eve had had prepared. He could remember none of the people whose hands had pressed his hand. He barely recalled Teddy finally saying, "Let us take you home. Your hat, Byron." He did remember looking at his hat as though he'd never seen it before: what did one do with this oddly shaped object? Did one play with it? Hang it on one's wall?

Teddy had to find the key nestled in Byron's pocket, had to open the door, to finally make him sit down. He kept wandering from room to room looking for Vanessa. She seemed to be running ahead of him, as in some frustrating dream, always just out of sight. But she was clearly in the house; evidence of her was everywhere—the daisies, bachelor buttons, and carnations in the vase by the front window, the roses in the garden behind the house, her muddy torn shawl . . . Byron picked it up, as though it were a clue to her, but Teddy pried it gently from his hands and sat him down.

"A tragedy like this," Teddy said, and stopped.

"It happened so quickly," Byron said.

"No time at all to prepare," Teddy said. "Byron . . ."

"A minute ago we were here, and then the church, and now we're back again. You've got to help me find her, Teddy."

Byron rose and walked into the living room. Dozens of canvases filled with images of Vanessa stood stacked against a wall. On the easel was a sketch pad Byron flipped through, each page another charcoal sketch of her. "Go home, Teddy," he said. "You've got your family to take care of."

"She's alive in these paintings, Byron. She'll always be just as you saw her. You'll never have to suffer her illness or her aging. You need never be without her."

"Go home, Teddy," Byron said.

"Maybe you should come with me," Teddy said. "Eve would be so happy to have you with us."

"Afraid for me, Teddy?" Byron said mildly, turning away from Vanessa. "Afraid I won't make my opening at The Colman? Remember, an artist is always worth more dead than alive."

"That's just the sort of half-cracked remark which worries me," Teddy said. "God, Byron. I'm *so* sorry about Vanessa, we all are, don't you understand? But Vanessa's dead now, and you're not. And next month you'll show Pissarro, Cézanne, and Manet that American painting is more than just another Hudson Valley landscape, more than just another portrait of George Washington crossing the Delaware."

Byron smiled wanly. "Go home. I'll be all right. I just want to be alone with her, you understand?" He walked unsteadily to a small mahogany chest set under a window, swung open the doors, and took out a full bottle of vodka.

"That won't help," Teddy said.

"Just let me be for a few days, won't you, Teddy? Just let me do what I have to do. Please?"

Even before Teddy had gone, Byron began to arrange the paintings, against the wall, leaning precariously on the shelves of the bookcase, on the easel, and then surrounding him in the chair. Everywhere he looked, he saw Vanessa. He tilted the bottle of vodka and took a long, deep swallow.

The faces bending over him were blurry, swirling as if they were water being sucked down a drain. His head ached horribly. What had happened? Slowly he began to make out Teddy, and the black-frocked figure of a man who could only be a doctor. With him was an angel all in white. A nurse? Had he fallen and cracked his skull? Then he remembered piling the paintings, pouring the vodka, striking the match. He groaned and turned on his side. The doctor was talking.

"He'll be all right, Mr. Shearing. A case of melancholia, not at all unusual in a situation such as this. He needs bed rest and then, if I may be so bold, I think a few months in the sanitarium. He needs to turn his attention *away*, if you understand. He's not in need of any medication I could prescribe. It's his soul which needs mending."

He heard the door close, and someone approach the bedside. Was it Vanessa? He turned, and Teddy peered down at him. "What have you done?" Teddy said, his voice level, without sympathy.

"I was drunk and . . . "

"I've called it off, everything, the critics, the buyers. I've had to cancel the invitations." He opened his hand, revealing a black smudge of ashes.

Byron tried to sit up and couldn't. He closed his eyes against the ashes, against Teddy. "I knew what I was doing," he said.

"It matters very little now. Just thank God you didn't hurt yourself. Once you're recovered you can start painting again."

"I don't think so, Teddy. I'm not of a mind ever to paint again."

"Oh, really! Just like that—it's not like you, this tantrum of self-pity."

"I'm not feeling sorry for myself. It's . . . Whatever it was compelled me to paint died when Vanessa died."

"Byron, listen. Dr. Lodge says you'll feel better after you rest. Don't make any more rash decisions. I know what you're capable of. You don't have any choice in the matter; those talents aren't yours to turn on and off like a lantern."

"Perhaps you're right. But I don't think so, Teddy. Anyway, as you said, I need more time. Just let me be for a while."

Teddy paused at the door; his face was very stern. "I'm sorry to say this, Byron, but I think it's true. Two fine people are dead today. Of the two, yours is the greater loss." He closed the door, making the wooden frame rattle. Byron stared at the blank wood for some time, blank as all the canvases in the world.

When he was intoxicated, it was easier to believe that Vanessa had gone for a walk, or a ride, or was visiting with Elsa Scott in Derry. He kept her things around, as if they might lure her back from the dead. But as the months went by, the stubborn fact of her absence remained, and it took more and more alcohol to drown that awareness. Byron, once an aficionado of Amontillado or port, soon found his taste was of far less importance than his loss of consciousness. And it became a task he undertook with great seriousness each morning. He'd push his way into wakefulness and reach for the bourbon. The roses faded and disappeared, the chrysanthemums too, and the Queen Anne's lace turned brown in the New Hampshire fields he'd walked through with Vanessa. By the time the snow was falling, he was a serious drunk. And he had not begun to paint again.

One afternoon, unshaven, disheveled, dirty, and despairing—the last of the bourbon had been finished not half an hour earlier—he went on a mad search of the house, pulling clothes from drawers, pans and pots from kitchen shelves, bed linen from the closet in the hall. Then he dimly remembered having hidden a bottle of something in his studio, the one room into which he almost never went. He opened cabinets and drawers, strewing tubes of paint and brushes around him, and in his haste he knocked over the bottle he was searching for. It fell to the floor, and Byron's heart stopped, but it hit a throw rug and, instead of shattering, began to roll across the slightly tilted floor, coming to rest before a stack of stretched canvas.

Something in the stack caught Byron's eye, and as he pawed through the canvases he came upon the painting of Vanessa in the garden, tall, poised, and inexpressibly beautiful among the long-stemmed red and yellow roses. He carried the portrait, dappled with sunlight, to the living room where his empty easel still stood. The smell of summer wafted into the room. Byron held his breath, and then the pain he'd been so good at dulling returned full force. How could he continue without her?

He found a box of matches and struck one but it broke in his unsteady hand. The second match went out before he could bring it to the canvas. He opened the bottle of bourbon, took a deep swallow, and put it down; as he struck the third one, he was so off-balance that the entire box fell to the floor, scattering matches everywhere.

He fell backwards into a chair, sobbing, calling out to Vanessa, who stood still among the roses, holding her parasol as if she caught his voice but paid no attention. "I need you," Byron sobbed. "I need you here with me. Come home, Vanessa. Please come home." And then his medication took effect; as he had every day for months now, Byron Sullivan passed out.

When he awoke it was morning, and as he groped abstractedly for his bottle, he was paralyzed with wonder. Winter sunlight streamed through the windows, and he could swear he heard birdsong. The room was filled with the smell of roses, an odor almost suffocating in its intensity. He looked around the room, trying to focus. Everywhere he looked, empty bourbon bottles stood upright, half-filled with clear water. And every bottle held a half-dozen long-stemmed American beauties, freshly cut. Red and yellow, they seemed more vibrant than anything he'd ever seen, so bright, in fact, the colors hurt his eyes. He struggled to his feet and stumbled toward his easel. He brought his face so close to the canvas his lips almost touched it.

There were no roses in the canvas, just hundreds of cut stems. And around them stood the garden, a stand of poplar trees under a bright sky. "Vanessa," he yelled. For she was nowhere to be seen.

He turned around as his heart began to race, sensing a

presence behind him. Almost afraid to look, he went to the French windows which overlooked the garden.

Twirling the parasol she'd held last summer, Vanessa stood, poised and tall and motionless, wearing her lacy ribbon-bedecked dress, warm as summer in the harshness of the winter landscape. Through the windows he called her name and she turned, barefoot as always, and smiled. He bolted from the room, knocking over the piano bench on which they'd sat so often, and burst through the back door. He ran to the spot where he'd seen her stand, and then realized he was slashing through drifts of snow in his worn trousers. The winter air stung his throat as he took and held a deep breath. He was alone—no birds, no parasol, no footprints in the snow, only the harsh whine of the wind. He turned, chilled to the heart, and ran back to the house. In the living room, the roses were gone. Empty liquor bottles lay strewn on the floor. The painting of Vanessa, as though it had never moved or changed, sat on the easel silently.

It happened again. The next day, pained to find the Brahms she'd been playing the day he returned from Teddy's with the news, he lit it and carried it to the living room, resolved to burn the painting. But she wasn't in the canvas; she'd fled again, this time leaving the roses behind her, and when he glanced up, he caught her reflection in the mirror on the wall. He turned, and there she was in the garden, twirling the parasol, up to her knees in snow. He picked up a chair and threw it through the windows, and calling, "Vanessa, I'm coming," he slipped through the shattered glass into the winter landscape. This time he kept his eyes on her and as he drew closer, she began to disappear, like one of those new-fangled photographic images in reverse. His heart beat wildly in his chest, and his voice was desperately calm.

"Where are you now?" he asked. "Where do you go? Are you somewhere out here lost, or is it I who's lost?" The snow drifted before him, pushed by the useless wind. "I must be mad," he said. Behind him, caught on canvas, Vanessa stood serene.

That night, at three, he was awakened by the sound of laughter. Around him the house was pitch black; he stood and stumbled into the hall. The bedroom door was closed, but a bright band of light seeped out from under it. He wrenched the door open and was greeted by sunlight streaming through the window across the floor, warming Vanessa who sat curled on the white wicker couch reading a book which obviously delighted her. Behind him the night was dark as ever night was. He moved toward her but as he did, she began to shimmer and fade, and afraid of losing her, he stopped. The scene was so familiar yet so odd, it took him a minute to remember. " 'A Summer's Day,' " he said. He turned, abandoned her to her reading, and ran back into the darkness.

He found a candle and lit it, and using it to guide him he slowly made his way up the spiral staircase to the second floor. He flung open the door of the first room he came to, and then the closet door, but what he was looking for eluded him. He searched the other rooms up there, and then, in a frenzy, he made his way to the chill, dark attic cluttered with boxes of books.

He found it, finally, a bright canvas done in whites and beiges, browns and golds, a study of sunlight and parquet, a portrait of Vanessa curled on a wicker couch reading a book. He'd put it away because it was to have been a surprise for her, and then he'd forgotten it, as he became immersed in other canvases, other portraits of her. He blew out the candle and wiped the sweat from his cheeks. Holding it like a shield, he began to make his way downstairs, sure at last of what he had to do.

Though attendance was by invitation only, the Byron Sullivan show at The Colman Gallery was so crowded it was difficult to see the paintings. All other works had been removed for this event, and still the walls were full. If one ignored the people one should talk to, the people one should meet, if one dedicated all one's time to viewing the paintings, it was difficult to see them all. Still, the effort was worthwhile.

For the recent work of Sullivan exceeded the glowing publicity which had been mounting for months. It was June, and even the New York air was heavy with the smell of roses and honeysuckle. And it was difficult to know if the smells were natural, or a result of the overwhelming impression the paintings gave.

Here was Impressionism with a difference: for along with the play of light and the sound of color, these paintings had a subject—the artist and his wife. In one Sullivan and the late Vanessa Winthrop walked hand in hand through a garden of roses. In another, they stood embracing against the trunk of an oak, while around them the wind and sun whipped the tall grass to a froth. They could be seen in Venice, in Rome, but mostly in and around their home near Derby, New Hampshire. There were paintings of an almost unbearable intimacy; in one the artist painted himself standing behind his wife

as her fingers moved over the keys of a grand piano, and
the closeness of the two, the tenderness with which
Sullivan's hands were poised above Vanessa Winthrop's
hair almost made one doubt the loves he'd had. In another, a rather brazen canvas, the couple was entwined
among the tangled sheets of a brass bed.

The artist stood with his longtime friend and agent
Theodore Shearing, a bit stunned by the unanimity of
the critical response.

"I've never seen you looking so well, my boy. You've
bounced back as I hoped you would, but given your
state for a while, this is nothing short of a miracle,"
Shearing said.

"It *is* a miracle," Sullivan said.

"This sudden outpouring. My God. It's simply con-
founding."

"But you said it yourself the day of the funeral,"
Sullivan said. "She lives in my work."

Shearing drew close and whispered, "You'll be
bloody rich, Byron. I hope you won't let money stifle
your passion to create."

Sullivan smiled and touched his friend on the elbow.
"No need to worry about that," he said. "No amount
of money could keep me from what I'm planning to
do."

Perhaps the most curious painting in the show was
one in which the viewer, if not careful, could get very
lost. For it seemed to be an impressionistic representation of the very place in which he stood. It was a canvas
of an art show, crowded with people, hung with paintings of the paintings around him. The artist was quite
clearly in the canvas, with his back to the viewer. And
he stared at a painting of himself staring at a painting,

as in a mirror tunnel. Behind him, in all the paintings and paintings of paintings, stood a mysterious woman in a black dress and veil, with a hat of red and yellow roses. And if one stared and stared it seemed this figure moved, came close to Byron Sullivan, and took his hand.

GUILT TRIP
by Steven Bauer

Based on the Universal Television series *Amazing Stories*
Created by Steven Spielberg
Adapted from the episode ''Guilt Trip''
Written by Gail Parent and Kevin Parent

I MEAN, I'D BE HAPPY TO TELL YOU THE STORY OF MY life and all that Holden Caulfield kind of crap if you were really interested, but first off I know most of you don't care a fig, although you'd pretend to, and second, I don't know very much about *who* my parents are. I've tried to do some research as any adopted kid might, but when you come from a family of emotions as big as mine, it's difficult to sort everything out. You might say my father was kin to Envy and my mother to Sorrow; then again you might say my father was Knowing Right and my mother Doing Wrong. But I think it's a lot more complicated than any of that, and besides, that's not the story.

You see, I'm Guilt, and though most of you don't recognize me by sight, I bet there aren't many of you out there who haven't heard my voice in your ear or felt the rough tips of my fingers tickle the hairs on your neck. And many of you have lain awake in the dark, your hearts pounding, in long and intimate conversation with me. For those of you in need of quiet prompting in public places, well, that can be arranged too.

51

Like Larry Minsk, can you hear me, Larry? You were at the Schooners Restaurant the other night, sitting alone in a back booth as always, though why you frequent that place I'll never know—lots of pin spots and framed drawings of antique cars, acres of blond wood polyethylened to a high gloss, and hanging overhead, a canopy of spider plants and asparagus ferns, always tickling your neck when you walk by. You had the Big Boy's Platter, the sixteen-ounce slab of prime rib, and you ate all the fat, too, didn't you, Larry? And you asked for both butter and sour cream on the baked potato. You even managed to put down a full bottle of a very reputable Stag's Leap cabernet. Who knows what you might have done if I hadn't arrived on time?

I loved the look on your face—my brothers Fear and Greed would have been bursting their buttons. When that nice young waiter removed the heavy silver top from the dessert tray, there I was, in miniature, right next to the strawberry cheesecake. "Hi there," I said. "You want to talk fattening?"

"Get off my sweets," you said, Larry, you old dog, and swatted at me as though I were a fly.

"You're going to Florida this winter?" I said. "How do you suggest getting into your bathing suit? You can only ask so much of rayon."

"I'll just have a bite," you pleaded. "Two at the most."

That's when I did my little flaming number, like a Crêpe Suzette, sending spears of fire from my fingers, sparks from the soles of my feet, until I was full size (though not as large as you, Larry) and sitting beside you in the booth. You'd picked up weight since last I tried to hold you down.

"Think of the homeless in America," I said. "Think of Africa. Think of the poor starving children in Asia, no joke."

"I need my strength," you said.

It was time to get abusive. "You're fat, Larry," I said. "You sit down in shifts." When our struggle resulted in the cheesecake flying to the floor and you diving after it, I said, very loudly, "How many calories in dinner? Let me count the ways." Next time, expect my sister, Shame.

Then I was sitting on your chest, trying to hold your hands down as you twisted and writhed, sticking out that enormous tongue of yours toward the cheesecake. "Pigs are one of my favorite animals," I said. "That's why I'd never call you a pig. Are you aware that as you lie here your mother is in a nursing home eating nothing but Jell-O?" I whispered in your ear.

"All right," you said. "All right." You were exhausted by then, to be sure, but I expect you to stick by your resolve to eat nothing but roughage and fruit, or I'll be back. I knew I'd done my job, because as I left, Larry, you were sitting in the booth again, waving away coffee, waving away the mints. Your face was longer, your eyes sadder: you were on your way to a good character-building depression.

Sounds like fun to you? I've got everything you've ever wanted, right? If you were me, you'd be powerful, you could change in size, and you could light your cigars with your fingers, that is if you wanted to ignore the Surgeon General's warning, and didn't mind leaving orphans behind.

But think of it this way for a minute. How would *you*

like it if all you did every minute of every day was spoil people's fun? Imagine this: you walk into a bar to do your job, calm as you please, whistling a Cole Porter tune, and wearing your new London Fog. You look good; you should bring a smile to people's faces. But what happens? One by one as you pass, the cigarettes get stubbed out; the couple in the corner celebrating their anniversary stops kissing and decides *against* the champagne—they'll settle for a glass of the house Chablis. The nice-looking woman at the bar suddenly covers her legs with her sweater when you say, "Your skirt is too short. Are you in the advertising business?"

It makes a fellow mean-spirited. I even developed this trick. I sit at the bar nice and quiet, minding my own business, until everyone's having a great old time —laughing, hitting one another on the back, telling raunchy jokes, ordering more rounds, smoking, screaming . . . and then I spin around and growl. Panic ensues, of a particularly underhanded and subtle sort: blushes show through even the most expert makeup jobs; everyone puts down his drink, and all the cigarettes go out like electric lights being switched off. The noise level falls below hearing; the barkeep turns down the jukebox. And half the patrons excuse themselves for the Men's or Women's Rooms, there to search their bloodshot eyes and dissipated faces for some semblance of propriety, some evidence of virtue. None, I gleefully know, for Guilt has them all by the throat. Though it's a good game, and one I'm an expert at, as you might imagine, after a while it's enough to turn a man sour.

So I drink too much occasionally, because it's a rough job ruining people's fun. I'd had quite a run of Scotches and had stumbled to the Men's Room the other night (just to pee, mind you; I'm *loaded* with virtue) when my beeper went off. "Guilt alert, one two eight Sycamore. Teenagers on couch, heavy petting." I'm a good boy, so I did what I was told; *flames from my fingers and flames from my toes, there's sure to be fire wherever Guilt goes.* Whammo! One twenty-eight Sycamore, a quiet split-level. There I was; insta-travel is the perq I like most.

A fire burned cheerily in the living room; with my skewed and bleary vision it looked for a moment as though the couch cushions were moving. I shook my head and hurried up the carpeted stairs to the second floor. I opened one door so fast I almost fell on my face. I found what I was looking for on my second try.

There he was, balding and rather chubby, mumbling like a bee around the stem of the girl's neck; her hair was up in curlers, and her skin looked pretty worn for a teenager's. Something was wrong with this picture, so I said, "This is wrong."

The man stopped kissing and looked at me in astonishment. So did the woman. "Oh, my God," she said. "I haven't seen you in years."

"You kids should be feeling really Gil-Tee."

"I understood when you showed up in the back of the Pinto, but we're *married* now." Kids today, such cheek. In the fifties, all it took was a brief appearance and then on to somewhere else. This one would require a little extra work; I took out my army training film projector and splashed the wall with some pretty horrid pictures. "Is that a *rash*?" the woman asked. That's when my beeper went off again.

•   •   •

I'd been recalled, you see, by the Big Guy. He's the Assistant to the Boss, but we've been on friendly terms for hundreds of years. His title was carved on his door in gold and he had primo pile carpeting, made of 100% virgin cloud. Beautiful furniture, the best. If I'd visited this guy on earth, I could have made him feel guilty about the luxury in no time. "Well, hello," he said. "Come in. Sit down. Guilt, it's good to see you, kid. You're one of my favorite emotions."

Impeccably tailored white linen suit; a maroon and blue rep tie, very classy. Dark glasses. What I really coveted was the white telephone on his desk, the direct line to . . .

"Nice to see you, Big Guy," I said. I adjusted my tie. I straightened the creases in my pants.

"Sit," he said. I sat. "First, let me tell you you're doing a good job, a fine job. For the most part you've made the world a guilty place to live. More and more people are feeling worse and worse." He checked some papers on his desk. "Those AT&T commercials are really working. People still aren't calling, but they're feeling more guilty about it. And Lean Cuisine sales are up; you know that's a division of Celestial Foods. I really have to commend you."

"We do what we can," I said humbly. Maybe this was my promotion.

"Any progress with Nixon?"

"None at all, sir. He's a tough nut to crack; I think he may actually lack a conscience. Won't budge an inch, even in his memoirs." I made my face a mask of jowly wrinkles and grunted from the upper chest, "*I am not a crook.*"

"Kissinger?"

"No luck," I said. "None with Gorbachev; none with Duarte; none with Qaddafi."

He waved his hand at me to make me stop. "Let me just get your opinion on something. What happened over on Sycamore?"

"Just now?" I asked. "Routine—kissing teenagers. I handled it."

"Have you been drinking?" he asked.

"No," I said. He looked hard at me; he always could see right through me. "Yes," I said. "What's the matter? Wrong house?"

"Right house," he said. "Wrong room. The two you were supposed to torture were on the living room couch. The couple you interrupted have been happily married for twenty-five years."

"To each other?" I asked.

"And that film you showed. From the Second World War? They probably won't get back together for eight months."

"I *thought* he was prematurely bald."

The Big Guy shook his head. "You're one of the best Guilts we've ever had, but recently you've been screwing up. Ruining the wrong people's lives, wasting your time on peccadillos." My head was beginning to spin. "I want you to take a vacation," he said.

Thank God, I thought, and looked up at the ceiling; for a minute I'd been sure he was going to demote me, or worse. "But I was just beginning to get through to Joan Crawford's daughter," I said meekly.

"I'm not making a suggestion. I'm giving an order. You have to go and have fun. Relax. Take a load off. Rethink the true seriousness of guilt."

"Fun?" I said, stretching it out into two syllables.

I'm afraid it was a bit of a whine. "Okay, okay. But *please* don't send me to one of those tropical places with fungus and warm fruit."

That's how I wound up on the boat. But try as I might, I just couldn't relax. When you've been working without a day off for hundreds of years, it gets to be a habit. I'd enter the dining room and everyone would step back from the buffet; people would take out their charge slips and add them up; I'd make couples in deck chairs suddenly see visions of sweatshops and foreign labor. I'd walk up behind a nice-looking gentleman who stood earnestly conversing with a woman and he'd say, "All right, all right. I'm married and my wife thinks I'm on a business trip."

When the maître d' tried to take me to my table, I said, " 'Bonjour, monsieur' yourself. Who do you think *you're* kidding? You're from Sandusky. If you can live with it, okay. Personally, I would have slit my wrists by now." He left me quickly enough.

At the piano bar I introduced myself as Harvey Pinkerton.

"We're the Beckermans," an elderly woman said. "Sam just retired and this is the first time we've been away since his bypass."

"I hope you're watching your cholesterol," I said.

"And I'm Judy McKay, and this is my husband Bob," another woman said. "Isn't this all marvelous?"

"Let's try to enjoy ourselves until the bills come," I said. "The kids can find another way to get to college."

Then I saw her—the most beautiful woman I'd seen in quite some time, maybe since the eighteenth century. She stood alone, leaning on the piano with an expres-

sion of such bliss I was momentarily without words.
When I walked over toward her, she gradually looked at
me.

"You're lovely," I said.

"Yes," she said. "I am."

"And you can take a compliment," I said.

"That's not what I meant," she said. " 'Lovely' is
my name."

"Your mother took quite a risk," I said. "What if
you'd wound up looking like Winston Churchill, or had
a mustache, or been Boris Karloff?"

"I've always been attracted to Boris in a spooky kind
of way," she said.

We had dinner. We had cream of asparagus soup,
Oysters Rockefeller, Lobster l'Americaine, a bottle of
Mumms' with dinner, and a bottle of Rémy Martin
after. Yes, we were full; yes, I was a little drunk, but
mostly on being with Lovely. She was toying with her
mousse, and I was lying as best I could, trying to make
up for the fact that I was centuries old, though I looked
no more than fifty. "When I left Harvard," I said, "my
Phi Beta Kappa key was glistening in the Massachusetts
sun, and rows of Cliffies wept . . . "

"Maybe we should go on deck," Lovely said.

"But you haven't finished your dessert," I said.

"I'm not hungry."

"You're wasting perfectly good food," I said.

"You're trying to make me feel guilty, but it won't
work. I'm here to have a good time and you're not
going to stop me." She smiled sublimely.

"You're beautiful when you're embarrassing me," I
said.

"No," she said. "Not beautiful. Just very, very pretty."

That's when the struggle began. We went on deck and stood looking out over the moonlit water. "This is wonderful," I said. "But think of the money this cruise cost and what it could do for the earthquake victims in Mexico City."

"One can help others and still have a good time oneself," she said. An ace. Fifteen-love.

The next day we were sitting taking the sun on deck. "Don't you feel we should be doing something other than just *sitting*?" I asked.

"No," she said. "I find the warmth positively exhilarating. Besides, sitting is one of the best things someone can do. It frees one from walking around." Thirty-love.

That night we were dancing. "Don't you think this is frivolous?" I said.

"Dancing is wonderful exercise," she said. " 'If music is the food of love, play on.' " Forty-love.

And yet another night. She was wearing a shimmering red dress and we were kissing so deeply and for so long it seemed we should both have died of suffocation. I tried to make her worry one last time, though my serve was admittedly weak. "Aren't you worried about your breath?" I asked.

"Not at all," she said. "I've always had perfect hygiene. Let me take you to my cabin."

"Aren't you afraid of diseases?"

"I don't worry about things like that. I live for the passionate moment."

"But what if I don't respect you afterwards?"

"The important thing is that I respect myself. And I

will, if I'm very, very good." Game point. Set point. Match point.

I fell in love. I hadn't gotten to her at all, though I wasn't—let's face it—at the top of my game. And I started to forget about feeling guilty myself. I can't tell you how uncomfortable that was.

Later I found out what happened in my absence; the Big Guy told me. Ice cream sales soared; there was a riot near the Häagen Dazs display at a Kroger's in Oxford, Ohio. Catholics simply *stopped* going to confession. A diocese near Chicago ran a TV spot in which a smiling priest said, "So come on down. Three priests, no waiting." Elderly people were abandoned in great numbers on the thresholds of nursing homes. Pregnant right-to-lifers showed up at abortion clinics. And applications to the school for Jewish Mothers dried up to nothing. It was, let me tell you, refreshing to know I'd truly been making a *dif*ference.

So I got the call, through my beeper, to wind it up and get back to work. I had twenty-four hours. Usually I'd have wanted to go, of course; before I'd met Lovely, the thought of going on vacation had caused palpitations. Now I didn't care so much. But I knew it was all over between us. I just didn't know how to tell her.

I was sitting at the bar nursing a Perrier and lime when she floated into the room, all in silver, like an angel. She sat beside me, touched my cheek with the longest, coolest fingers in the world, and I could see tears in her eyes.

"What's wrong?" I said.

"Could we . . . could we go up on deck and talk?" she said. "I have a few things to tell you."

"I have some things to tell you too," I said. "Some small, teeny, insignificant things that shouldn't ruin your life."

There was a moon, of course, though the water was rough, and for a while there I didn't know if I was literally going to spill my guts.

She touched my hand and sighed and looked away and sighed, like every bad movie you've ever seen. "I feel so badly about something," she said. "So guilty."

For just a moment I had to admit to pride. "I did that to you," I said. "Mea culpa."

"No," she said. "I haven't been totally honest with you. I'm not who you think I am. I'm not even a person."

Now I had been to bed with this non-person and I knew she was a person. She was distraught and I tried to calm her. "Look," I said. "Some of my best friends aren't people. None of it matters. I'm in love with you."

"That's just the problem," she said. "I don't know if you're in love with love or with me because I don't know whether you're in love with what I am—which is Love—or with just the idea of being in love—which is what I *do*. Do you know what I'm trying to tell you?"

"Not yet," I had to admit.

"I'm Love," she said.

"You're *Love*?"

"I know it sounds crazy, but I just run around and make people fall in love. That's why I spend a lot of my time on cruise ships."

"I can't believe it," I said. The truth was, I couldn't believe it. I mean, here we were both working for the same organization and it looked like we'd fooled each other.

"I'll prove it to you," she said. "Pick out any two people—make it hard—and I'll get them to fall in love before your eyes." I looked around; in the corner, wielding a cane, was a middle-aged woman stout enough to play Brünnhilde in *The Ring*. And coming down a stairway was a terribly slender, even effeminate young man who looked like a college senior majoring in engineering.

Lovely blew a kiss first to him and then to her. The two of them stopped in their tracks, looked around as if searching for the bee which had bitten them, and when they saw one another, they started running—get this, *in slow motion*—and I swear I heard these tremulous violins. Daisies could have sprouted from the deck. When they reached each other, cymbals crashed, the violinists sawed away like crazy, and fireworks exploded in the black sky. I must have looked impressed because Lovely said, "Then you don't mind that I lied to you?"

"I lied to you too, my dear," I said, gallantly as I could.

"You mean you can't make love nine times in a night?"

"Oh," I said, blushing. "That was just a little white lie. But, you see, I'm not a nuclear physicist. I'm . . . I'm Guilt."

"Guilt?" she said, drawing back, genuinely shocked. "Like when little kids get bad grades on their report cards and their mothers cry and hide in the bathroom?"

"Yes," I said. I'd been proud of that one.

"You're kidding, aren't you?" she said.

"You need proof? Pick out anyone and let me at him."

She looked around and saw a man, dressed in a tux, red-cheeked, in perfect health, whistling, a man without a care in the world. She nodded at him, and I went to work. I walked over, put my arm around him and said, "I know what you did to your partner and you should be ashamed of yourself." Instantly his cheeks turned ashen, his eyes grew dark, and his shoulders sank. He began hitting himself on the chest and he turned to the rail and yelled, "Murray, Murray, I couldn't help it. My writing is sloppy. I wrote a one and it looked like a seven; no, no, it *was* a seven. It was Bernice, Murray, she wanted diamonds, furs." He tried to throw himself overboard but two stewards rushed forward and restrained him. I walked back to her, smiling.

But she wasn't impressed. Her arms were crossed and her eyes shone with malice. "So you're Guilt," she said. "I think that's terrible."

"Hey," I said. "Wait a minute. Let's not get too judgmental here. Did I give *you* a hard time?"

"But I'm something nice," she said.

"I'm working my way up," I said. "I was adopted. I put in for Loyalty, but it was taken. Guilt's a dirty job, but someone has to do it. And it hasn't been easy."

"I'm sorry," she said. "Part of my problem is I always get critical when I start to get close. I'm lousy at Commitment."

"Nice girl," I said. "I met her at a wedding."

Lovely turned away now, gripping the rail with her lovely hands. Below us the sea rolled and rocked. "Maybe we should just think of this as a perfect week when we found each other, loved each other, and let go before anyone had to seek professional help."

"You mean just end it?" I said. She shook my hand and walked away. I mean, I felt terrible.

We docked the next day and I knew it was back to work, and that I'd better be good after the vacation the Big Guy had sent me on. But I couldn't get my mind off her.

I was about to get into a taxi and make my way to a funeral, any funeral, when I saw her; she was running toward me, and it wasn't slow motion. Were there violins? Who could tell? My heart, old as it is, was pounding. We hugged. We kissed. "You want to hear something crazy?" she said. "I really love you."

"I love you too," I said. "But how will I do my job? I'll feel awful having to divide my time between work and home."

"It'll be great," she said. "You can take care of the kids. What you do best is what they need. Besides, what's Love without Guilt?"

"I work during meals," I said.

"I work on Saint Valentine's Day, and I'm *really* busy in June."

I shrugged; who cared? Maybe this would be good for me. Maybe I'd be easier on mortals after this. "You know," I said, "this could be the beginning of a beautiful friendship." There were no airplanes around, but the fog was seeping in as it should have. I thought of all of them dead—Bogart, Bergman, Lorre, Greenstreet. Michael Ruiz and Paul Henreid and even Dooley Wilson.

But I, I was still alive, after hundreds of years. And *boy,* did *I* feel guilty.

MR. MAGIC
by Steven Bauer

Based on the Universal Television series *Amazing Stories*
Created by Steven Spielberg
Adapted from the episode ''Mr. Magic''
Written by Joshua Brand and John Falsey

Lou Bundles had been performing for fifty years and still he felt the back of his neck prickle and his heart pick up tempo. Out front, the patrons of the Magic Castle were applauding the end of Nick Edmonds's act and in a minute Lou would have to take his place before them as they sat at their small, square, cloth-draped tables. A new guy was on lights, a kid who'd just begun a week ago, and his cues were off and his spots were misdirected. The night before, they'd shone directly into Lou's eyes so he couldn't see the audience. He straightened his tie and adjusted his sleeves as if he were about to undergo a job interview.

Next to him, Murray Tropicana, the owner and emcee of the Magic Castle, cleared his throat, getting ready for the introduction. "What the hell's wrong with the lights, Murray?" Lou said. It wasn't what he wanted to say; what he wanted to say was that he was scared. Lately he'd been feeling a little shaky, but he couldn't admit it to this kid nearly thirty-five years younger than he was.

"Lights are fine, Lou," Murray said.

Oh, well, Lou thought. He poked Murray in the side with his elbow. "Got some live ones out there tonight, eh, Murray? I'm gonna give 'em the old saucers tonight; you know how they love that."

"Sounds great," Murray said. The crowds here were full of people, God bless them, who still wanted to believe in magic, special effects had taken the zing out of everything. Now they wanted to see guys like this David Copperfield who could make the Statue of Liberty disappear, not old guys like Lou Bundles with his card tricks and strings of handkerchiefs and pigeons out of hats. But in his day, Lou Bundles had been *some*thing.

"Make sure that new kid hits the spot on cue," Lou said. The frantic pulsing music came to a halt and the audience burst into applause as Edmonds sped past him, brushing the curtain, and Murray left him for the spots and the mike and the crowd. His heart was racing now.

"Thank you, Nick Edmonds!" Murray said. "And now, ladies and gentleman, a man who's performed here at the Magic Castle ever since we opened in 1932." Lou winced; how often had he asked Murray to change the introduction? "A warm welcome, please, for that master of prestidigitation—Mr. Lou Bundles!"

The music began racing again and Lou was out in the light now, smiling broadly, barely able to see where his feet were going to step, so blinding were the spots. Murray wandered out among the tables to watch as a customer would, and two tall slender women, in writhing fur boas, carried out his folding table, draped with a black cloth.

"Thanks, Murray," Lou said, squinting. Again tonight he couldn't see the audience. "You know, I knew Murray when his old man ran this place, and it's heart-warming to see he's kept up with the old ways. And the old wages." He smiled, waited for the laughter, and when the silence grew embarrassing, hurried on. The saucer trick wasn't difficult, but if the lighting was wrong . . .

"They say you can't teach an old dog new tricks," he said, "but who needs new tricks when the old ones are still the best." He pulled six saucers from under his coat and began throwing them out and shimmying, rotating his hips, making them whirl around his body. He caught one and tossed it in the other direction. He was just beginning to feel relaxed when the audience started fidgeting, he could feel them, and a wave of nervous laughter reached him. He looked up and could see, plain as daylight, the strings controlling the saucers; and if he could see them, he knew the audience could see them even more clearly. That damn kid on the lights. He'd have to talk to Murray, get the damn kid fired. In his haste to pull the saucers in, he mistimed, and two fell to the stage. There was a smatter of polite applause as he put them behind him, on the table, as quickly as possible. Time for the cards. They never let him down.

He pulled the deck out of his jacket pocket, shuffled them expertly, and then, shielding his eyes, he said, "I need a volunteer." He saw a woman close to the stage, middle-aged, not too beautiful, not too smart. "You, sweetheart," he said, pointing. "Come on up here." Like every volunteer he'd ever called, she pretended to protest as her husband urged her on, and then blushing with pleasure she stood beside him. He showed her the cards. "A regular deck, no? You check it over. Now you pick a card and show it to the audience, but I don't see it and don't tell me what it is."

She did as she was told and reinserted the card in the deck. "Now everyone, you remember that card." He gave the deck to the woman and told her to shuffle it. "Sweetheart, I'm going to hold the deck right here," Lou said, "and your card will rise like cream to the top." With his forefinger, he tapped the deck and cheerfully held up the first card. "There it is," he said.

But the woman looked uncomfortable and the audience began to laugh. "No, it's not," she said.

"What're you talking about it's not your card?" Lou said. Every now and then during the past few years he'd gotten a troublemaker which was why of late he'd always picked middle-aged women.

"No, it's not," she said. Lou felt suddenly confused. He looked at the card he'd held up, the seven of clubs.

"What was your card?" he asked.

"The ten of hearts."

"You sure?" Had he made a mistake? He turned slightly away from the lights so he could see better and began counting the cards. One and then another slipped away from him and fluttered to the stage. Hurriedly he waved his hands around the deck as if casting a spell —"Okay! Okay!" he said—and then he tapped the top card three times with his finger and flipped over the two of diamonds.

In his dressing room, he sat before the mirror, wiping off his makeup with cold cream. Around the mirror's edges, the yellowed newspaper clippings and photographs looked like dried leaves recently fallen from trees. There were pictures of him with guys like Sid Caesar, Jack Benny, George Gobel, and Phil Silvers back in the early days. A photo of him from his appearance on the Ed Sullivan Show, signed by Ed himself. News clippings about his acts—the time he made the entire bird cage disappear, with three finches and a cockatoo inside; the time he'd shuffled the deck of cards and then had made the cards arrange themselves numerically by suit.

There was a knock on his door and Murray entered, looking gloomy and forlorn. "Murray, Murray," Lou Bundles said. "How's the son of my best friend in the world, may he rest in peace? Went pretty well tonight, don't you think, all things considered?" He pulled at the cream on his cheek with a tissue. "Don't know if maybe you noticed but there were some problems with the lighting. What's the matter, you got some gas? Here," he said, rummaging through a drawer.

"Lou," Murray Tropicana said. "I gotta pull you, Lou."

"What?" Lou asked. He stopped rummaging and looked at Murray's reflection in the mirror.

"I can't let this continue."

Lou shrugged, tried to stay calm, though his heart had begun the old rumba. "All right, all right, you're right. I had an off night."

"I'm sorry, Lou, but it's not just tonight."

Lou stood up slowly, with as much dignity as he could muster. "You giving me the boot, Murray?" he said.

Murray shook his head and swatted the air between them. "I'd never do that, Lou. Long as I'm running the business, there'll always be a place for you."

"Charity you're offering me?" Lou said. "In the washroom you'll put me? A doorman maybe? You're wrong, Murray. My time's not up yet."

"I think maybe it is, Lou," Murray said. He was

looking at his pants now, as though there were insects crawling up his legs.

"You think?" Lou said. "You think? Your old man is turning over in his grave to hear you say what you just said to me right now. When my time is up I'll know it, I promise you that."

Murray slowly raised his eyes until Lou could see them again. "Okay, Lou. If that's what you say." He turned and left the dressing room, and in the brief second the door was open, a cold breeze blew in.

Joe's Diner was a throwback, like Lou Bundles himself. It was a good honest hashery, with cheap thick coffee and homemade soups and daily specials like the one Lou was eating—a pan-fried pork chop, mashed potatoes, and green beans for $2.35. Joe himself was as old as Lou, or nearly so, though he didn't look much over fifty, and Lou thought again, as he often had, how black men and women never seemed to grow old.

"Be a nice fella, Joe," Lou said, "and bring an old man a nice cold glass of water." The door opened and the bird whistle Joe had installed a few years back let out its wheezy, puny, high-pitched song. Lou turned to see Dora and Johnny Duncan, old friends, *old* friends of his come in as they did most every evening.

"Hi, Lou," Dora said. "How'd your show go tonight?"

"Not so good," Lou said.

"Lousy crowd," Johnny said. "Bastards can really get you."

"Crowd was great," Lou said. "I was lousy."

"Everybody has an off night," Dora said.

In the warmth of his friends' sympathy, Lou could feel the bubble of pain in his gut expanding until he knew he couldn't keep it in any longer. "Murray wants to put me out to pasture," he said indignantly. "Me! I got commendations from President Hoover, for crying out loud! I got mash notes from Doris Day and Ginger Rogers. I'm Lou Bundles, damnit." He could feel the blood pounding in his ears; Dora had reached out and now held his elbow. He shook off her hand and took a drink of the water Joe had brought him. "If I'm goin' out, I want to go out in style." His own self-pity caught in his throat and for a minute he thought he might cry at seeing how low he'd let himself fall, so low that he'd spill his guts in a public eatery.

The door's bird whistle let out a low moan and his friend Jack Greenberg entered, dragging another elderly man by his suede-patched elbow. "Lou," Jack said. "You got a minute? I got someone I want you to meet." The other man was standing before Lou now and Jack said, "Lou Bundles, this is my brother-in-law, Harry Stryker. Harry's a real big fan of yours."

Stryker's face was very red and his eyes were wide open, like someone who'd just received an electric shock. He stammered a little in embarrassment. "It's a real honor, Mr. Bundles. Nineteen forty-six, my wife Flora and me we took a vacation to Florida, Bellevue Arms Hotel, just to see you."

"You boys care to sit down?" Lou said. Jack remained standing, but Harry Stryker sat on the stool next to Lou, as though they were old pals. "Jack here tells me you're still *work*ing." He smacked himself on the forehead with his palm. "I can't believe I'm sitting here

having a legitimate conversation with the great Lou
Bundles. Me, Harry Stryker, from Teaneck, New Jersey.''

''Calm down, Harry,'' Jack said. To the others he
confided *sotto voce*, ''He's got a bad heart. Hey Lou,
think you could, you know, show us a little something?
For my brother-in-law?''

Lou's stomach tightened. He didn't have any magic
left in him, not even for his friends, not even for these
people who'd believe he could walk on water if he told
them he could.

''I don't know, Jack,'' he said. ''It's getting a little
late . . .'' But Dora and Johnny nudged him and
strangers from the booths started gathering round, and
the look on this Stryker's face was—well—a*dor*ing, so
he said, ''All right, all right.''

He placed a napkin over his knife and spoon, mumbled a little hocus-pocus, waved his left hand a couple
times, and whipped off the napkin with a flourish; the
knife and spoon were gone and in their place were two
forks. Everyone smiled and clapped. Lou replaced the
napkin, mumbo-jumboed some more, and this time
when he removed the napkin nothing was there. The
crowd, even his friends who'd seen him do this over and
over, even in the beginning when he'd messed it up and
let everyone see how it was done, gasped in amazement.

''Hey, Joe,'' he said. ''Someone's trying to steal your
silverware.'' He reached inside Harry Stryker's sport
coat and pulled out a knife, a spoon, and two forks.

The supply room of the Magic Castle was a warehouse of tricks and gags, the unwritten twentieth-
century history of magic. Dummies hung suspended

from the ceiling; the coffin-like boxes in which innocent young ladies were sawed in half straddled old saw-horses. Tuxedos with moth holes hung from rusting coat hangers, and the room was thick with scarves, capes, wands, balls, ropes, metal rings of all sizes, sequined costumes, and top hats. Lou wandered among the items, picking some up and absent-mindedly dropping them. He was hoping that being here would jar his memory, make him think of a trick he'd seen or heard of once, or remember one he used to do, something to prop up his sagging act. He needed help. Danny Morris, a nice enough kid from the Bronx, was with him, but like all these nice enough kids he was a little too big for his britches, not enough respect for his elders, he acted as though he'd invented magic, for crying out loud.

"Murray tells me you got yourself a two-week spot in Vegas," Lou said.

"Yeah," Danny said, shrugging it off.

"That's great, kid, great."

"I'll get you those balls, Lou," Danny said. He walked over to a chest on the far side of the room. Lou put his hands on his hips and took a deep breath. In here, magic smelled like mothballs, musty fabric, and wallpaper paste. Danny brought him the balls and he balanced them in his hands.

"Don't feel right to me," he said. "No sir, not like the ones we used to use."

"These are standard, Lou," Danny said, looking away. Damn kids had no respect.

"Standard for who?" he said. "For people under the age of twelve, you telling me? Look, I gotta put on one hell of a performance tonight—"

"Right, Lou. You mentioned that."

"Just so you know," Lou said.

"You need anything else?" Danny said, softening a little. "Lou?"

"Cards," Lou said. "I need cards." Danny reached into an old glass-topped display case where dozens of packs of cellophane-wrapped decks were stacked. "Not those," Lou said. "Not those cheap plastic things. They're what got me into trouble in the first place." He wandered over to another counter and peered through the glass. He could see his reflection and beyond it a deck of old cards. The queen of hearts was on the top, heartbreakingly Victorian in her costume and demeanor. "Gimme those," Lou said. They reminded him of cards he used to use. They were old cards; they'd been *used*. "How much?" he said.

"Murray says it's on the house," Danny said.

"Lou Bundles pays his own way," he said. "Two bits and we call it even?"

It was hot backstage, he thought. At any rate, Lou was sweating to beat the band, and the band was really making time. Murray was on stage saying, "The amazing Miss Jayne Anne Fips," as the music ended and the audience applauded. "And now, ladies and gentlemen, the Magic Castle is pleased to present—back by popular demand—the Master of Magic himself. Ladies and gentlemen, please, a warm round of applause for Lou Bundles."

Lou stumbled out to a scattering of hands. "Thanks, Murray," he said. "Tonight I think I've got something really special for you, at least I better, right, Murray?" Lou smiled, but no one else did. "You know, I knew Murray when his father ran this place and it's heart-warming to see Murray's kept with the old ways, and the old wages." At least tonight the lights weren't in his eyes; he could see the audience, but right now he wished he couldn't.

Things were falling apart around him, he could feel it. Sweat was sliding from his forehead into his eyes. He reached into his coat pocket for a handkerchief and mistakenly caught the tied silk scarves which cascaded to the floor in a rainbow of color as the audience began to laugh. "I got some tremendous magic for you tonight, ladies and gentlemen," he said, trying to stuff the scarves out of sight. A ball dropped from his sleeve and bounced across the stage. As he took a step after it, another ball fell from his other sleeve.

He bent over to catch it before it got away from him, and he could feel the tails of his jacket snag on the prop stick he had in the seat of his pants. A dove flew from the back of his jacket and made for the nearest exit. "Aw, for crying out loud," he said. "Somebody get that bird, will you?" The audience was howling now, and it suddenly occurred to Lou that he might turn a disaster into a triumph; he'd pretend he was a comedian, not a magician. He'd just continue to make a fool of himself as he had, and then leave the audience thinking that was what he'd intended.

But he wasn't a comedian, damnit, and he didn't want to make a fool of himself. He took a deep breath, reached up to feel his cheeks to see if he was as red with embarrassment as he feared. "Okay, okay," he said. "Settle down. Everything's under control now." This would be his last night; he knew it. Murray was going to skin him and nail his hide to the wall.

He fumbled in his pocket and pulled out the new deck

of cards. "I got a card trick for you," he said. "It's the amazing boomerang trick I first performed in . . ."

One of the cards, without his help, without his knowledge or participation, slipped from the middle of the deck, shot away from Lou Bundles, and hovered in the air over the audience, like a flat rectangular cloud. As the audience gasped in amazement, a second card shot free of the deck and joined the first card in the air. Lou looked at the audience; many jaws had come unhinged, something that happened pretty rarely, he could attest to that, and on Murray's face was a look approaching reverence. It was a pretty good trick, Lou thought. He wished he knew who was doing it.

The cards began dancing, began flying, zipping here and there like cartoon bluebirds, like the roadrunner and Wile E. Coyote, like two aerial gymnasts. They followed one another; they traded places. They did backflips and loop-de-loops and barrel rolls, and after about five minutes of stunned silence on the part of the audience beneath them, they came and hovered before Lou Bundles's eyes, as if they were privates and he the drill sergeant, as if they were clicking their heels together and coming to strict attention.

Without a word, he turned and walked off stage. Behind him, the cards followed in single file. The audience was on its feet, and the men and women were howling with awe now, not derision. One of the pretty young things in a feather boa stood stunned at the side of the stage. "Bring me a double bourbon," Lou said as he passed her. "A double double."

He awoke when the cat jumped on the bed and started rubbing his head against Lou's chin, as he always did when he was hungry. He was hung over and bleary-eyed, and he swatted at the cat with the back of his hand. "Beat it, Merlin," he said. "You got plenty of food in your bowl. Go look again." He turned over and saw the deck of cards he'd carefully removed from his coat the night before. Just a dream, he thought. What time was it? What *day* was it? He rubbed his eyes and sat up. Merlin ground the top of his skull against Lou's elbows and purred.

Lou picked up the deck and held it to his ear. He shook it and held it to his ear again. Nothing. He slowly opened the pack and two cards shot out and hovered in the air over the bed. Merlin stood on his hind legs and pawed at them.

As if in fear, they shot across the room until they clicked against the wall, then slid down to the floor, Merlin was off the bed and after them in no time.

"Hey, you, come here," Lou yelled at Merlin, but it wasn't the cat who obeyed. The cards zipped across the floor and wiggled next to Lou's slippers. He pulled his feet away from them as though they were a pair of vipers. "Get outta here!" he yelled. They shot back across the room.

His fear modulated to interest. "Come back here," he said. The cards scooted back. "Oh boy," he said. "Oboyoboyoboy."

"I was wrong," Murray said. "I'll say it again. I was dead wrong. You were incredible. You blew my socks off. What am I talking about—you blew everybody's socks off. Let me tell you something, Lou. You're at the top of your game. What am I talking about—you're at the tippy top of your game."

They sat in Joe's Diner, and Lou was having the special. "Brisket's very lean," he said.

"All right," Murray said. "Let's get down to business. Six shows a week, name your price. Two on Friday."

"I'm no spring chicken, Murray," Lou said.

"Fine, Lou. One show Friday, five shows a week. So how's your health? You drinking your prune juice? You need some cash?"

Lou pushed the air in front of him as though he were refusing a handful of bills. "Maybe you could slip me a few passes for my friends," he said.

"Done," Murray said. He reached across the table and Lou shook his hand. "So tell me," Murray said. "Is it wires?"

"Murray," Lou said.

"Some kinda remote control. Little batteries on the cards. Tiny little batteries."

"Murray," Lou said.

"Right," Murray said. "Sorry. It's magic, right?"·

"Right," Lou Bundles said. "It's magic."

"Good evening, ladies and gentlemen," Murray Tropicana said. "Welcome to the Magic Castle. We have a really terrific show for you tonight. We ask that you please don't smoke during this performance, but it wouldn't hurt if you ordered a few drinks. And now, without further ado, the moment you've all been waiting for. After fifty years, still the one, the only, the amazing Lou Bundles!"

The news had gotten around, and the place was packed. Lou's air was magisterial, calm, as he walked on stage. Dora and Johnny Duncan were in the audience, along with Jack Greenberg, Joe, Harry Stryker, and others he'd known for years, some of whom had never seen him perform. He quieted the audience with a wave of his hand.

"May we have a piano, please," he said. From stage right, two tall, slender women in white, shimmering costumes slit to the knee, their blonde hair piled high on their heads, pushed a baby grand toward Lou. From his coat pocket he removed the deck of cards, opened it, and flung the contents out over the heads of the audience. Instead of fluttering down among them, the cards hung where they'd been thrown, hovering over the upturned faces, fifty-two of them shimmering in the spotlights.

Lou turned his back on the cards but they didn't flinch. He tossed the tails of his tux behind him, sat down at the piano, and began to bang out the opening chords of Mendelssohn's Wedding March.

In the air over the audience, the cards came to attention from their various positions, and formed two single-file rows of twenty-six cards, headed by the queen and king of hearts. As Bundles kept playing, the two ranks slowly approached the piano, until they were inches away from the magician's head. He stopped playing and stood.

"Do you," he said, nodding to the Queen of Hearts, "take the King of Hearts as your lawfully wedded husband?" The card bent slightly in the middle, as if nodding. The audience broke into spontaneous applause, as though they'd doubted her intentions. "And do you," Bundles said, "take the Queen of Hearts to be your lawfully wedded wife?" he asked the king. The card nodded as the other had.

"Then by the power vested in me as your sole personal magician, I now pronounce you man and wife," he said. "You may kiss the bride." The two cards turned slowly toward one another in the air, pivoting as awkwardly and carefully as if they were carved figures in an intricate panorama timed to move and bow, to curtsy and kiss at noon and nine and three and midnight. There was awestruck silence as Lou Bundles himself, certainly not a carven figure, bowed low.

Joe's had been closed to everyone except regulars for a party in Lou's honor. All his friends who'd been at the Magic Castle were there, as well as others who hadn't made the show but who wouldn't have missed a party. Crepe paper streamed from the fluorescent lights, and the booths were loaded with party hats and noisemakers as if it were New Year's Eve.

"Give these folks anything they want, Joe," Lou Bundles said, "and put it on my tab."

"Hey, Lou, honey," Dora Duncan said. "How about a little magic for old time's sake?"

Lou was tired, and wanted to sit down; he wanted to have a drink and a couple of laughs. He'd done his performing earlier and tried to say no, but the crowd wouldn't take no for an answer, and finally he relented. He held out his hand as he had earlier at the Magic Castle, and the crowd grew silent. "You guys are the best bunch of friends an old man ever had," he said. "I could never say no to you."

He pulled out the deck, winked at Dora, blew on his fingers, selected a card at random, and tossed it out toward his friends. It fluttered to the ground, like any card would. "Hey you," he said, "get back up here."

The card didn't move. Lou mumbled, tossed another card, and watched as it too fell to the floor. Lou held up the deck and said, "Hey, you guys. What's wrong with you?"

"Take it easy, Lou," Dora said.

Johnny Duncan stooped and picked up the two cards. Lou tossed another one out, and it fell to the ground. "I don't get it," he said.

"It's all right, Lou," Dora said. "It doesn't matter."

"You're just tired, Lou," Jack Greenberg said. "You said so yourself."

"I don't know what's wrong with them," Lou said.

"They're old cards, Lou," Johnny said.

"Throw them away and get yourself a new bunch," Jack said.

"You don't know what you're talking about," Lou said. He grabbed at the cards Johnny had, and one of them ripped in half. He looked at it, thunderstruck. In one hand he held the head of the queen of spades, and in the other her intricate, jewel-bedecked neck. He had to get out of there; he needed the air.

Lou Bundles sat at the kitchen table, wearing reading glasses on the bridge of his nose. The cards were spread in front of him. With Scotch tape, Elmer's glue, and exquisite care he was mending the queen of spades, and touching up the others in the deck which had gotten bent, scratched, or nicked in the rough handling they'd received over the last several weeks.

"There now," he said. "All you guys needed was a little rest. Get a little older, it just takes a little longer. It's a good thing none of you had any broken bones." He sat back and crossed his arms. "I'm thinking of getting you guys a new wax job. Gonna have to do it myself if I want it done right. Don't know who to trust these days.''

He held up the queen of spades and showed her to the others which lay on the table, or leaned against the salt and pepper shakers, the sugar bowl, the jar of herring. ''There,'' he said. ''How's that look? All the stars in the sky don't look prettier than you guys when you're hanging in the air. I told Murray only once in a performance, you need your rest.''

He leaned backwards in the chair and picked up a brand-new leather card case from the counter. ''I got a surprise for you guys, so you can travel in style. Real genuine leather, $37.50. And I got a new idea for tonight. You ready? See, I sit down at the piano and start playing 'Autumn Leaves,' you know it?'' He stood up and waved his hands back and forth as though he were a hula dancer moving in a slow motion. '' 'The falling leaves,' '' he sang in his cracked husky voice, '' 'drift by my window, the autumn leaves, of red and gold.' Now you guys are going to make a maple tree, real New England, and then at a certain point you flutter to the ground, but instead of getting raked up you fly back into a springtime cherry blossom tree like in Washington. I'll make up some song about cherry blossom time, don't worry. Whaddaya think? Want to try it?'' Lou started singing ''Autumn Leaves,'' and the cards on the table vibrated, struggling against time and gravity. He sang louder and the cards tried harder, it seemed, shaking as if they had palsy.

''Come on,'' Lou yelled. ''Fly! Get up here. You're flying cards!'' But they lay still.

Lou stared at them as though they'd chosen to betray him. "You tricked me," he yelled. "A couple great shows so everyone thinks I got my magic back and that's it? So I can be an even greater fool? I don't need you. I been the amazing Lou Bundles for fifty years without you and I'm *still* the amazing Lou Bundles. Watch this."

He stalked to the refrigerator, flung open the door and grabbed three eggs. He had barely begun juggling when one of the three fell to the linoleum and splattered Lou's slippers. He grabbed another egg, kept juggling, and soon it had joined the scramble on the floor.

"You want some more magic?" he yelled as he grabbed a steak knife. "Now you see it, now you . . ." The knife which he'd tried to hide in the sleeve of his bathrobe clattered to the floor and he looked at the long bleeding scratch its serrated teeth had left on his wrist. The material world was turning against him. He stared at the cards for a moment, and they stared back, implacable as any deck of cards, without intelligence, feeling or spirit, fifty-two rectangles of plastic-coated paper with printed numbers and faces in two simple colors, black and red.

"Ladies and gentlemen," Murray Tropicana said, "I give you the one, the only, the amazing Lou Bundles."

Lou walked out to one of the largest ovations of his life. The cards were safely tucked in the jacket of his coat.

He'd done a lot of thinking since the morning. The cards were—there wasn't any other way to say it, they were *old*. They were still more beautiful, finely detailed, and individual than anything you could find today. Though their colors were a little faded, and their edges cracked and bent, you could still tell they came from a time when craft mattered. They had character. In fact, Lou had come to see, they were everything he'd ever hoped would one day be said about him. "Thank you very much, ladies and gentlemen," he said. Tonight his heart was very calm, and he felt not the slightest bit sweaty or nervous. He was a man at the height of his powers; he could tell. The audience hung on every word he said. "You know, when I was four years old I saw a magician pull a rabbit out of a hat and I said to myself, Lou, that's the life for you. And for the last seventy years magic has been my life and I've loved every minute of it. I've got memories, seen things and done tricks that other people can only dream about." The audience thought he was about to take them down memory lane, on a guided tour of the best tricks of the incomparable Lou Bundles.

"Magic is the greatest show on earth," he said. "And when a magician can no longer create magic, it's time for him to pack up. I realized today that time has come for me." He held up his hands toward the audience in the traditional gesture of disavowal. "I know you'll be kind and try to tell me no, but, well, you'll have to trust me. I'm sorry, folks, no tricks tonight; we're calling it quits while we're still on top."

He took the deck of cards from his pocket and held it up. "All fifty-three of us," he said. "Goodbye and God bless." Then he walked off stage. The audience sat silent in their seats, not knowing how to respond. Lou could only hope the cards had enough left in them for the last hurrah.

But he shouldn't have worried. As he opened the top, all fifty-two of them flew out on stage, and for the brief ten seconds before they flew off again to rejoin Lou, they spelled in large block letters before the dark velvet curtain the word

GOODBYE

THE MAIN ATTRACTION
by Steven Bauer

Based on the Universal Television series *Amazing Stories*
Created by Steven Spielberg
Adapted from the episode ''The Main Attraction''
Teleplay by Brad Bird and Mick Garris
Story by Steven Spielberg

He was in the Rose Bowl. The crowd was on its feet, roaring its approval. Hundreds of beautiful girls waved pompons and chanted his name as the card section flipped its placards to reveal the syllables to which the entire stadium now rocked in two-beat rhythm. Over the P.A. the announcer's slick voice tried to calm the crowd. "Your attention, please! As you know, we have a special guest with us today. A member of seven all-state squads in football, basketball, and baseball. The most popular student in his class. A great athlete and one helluva guy! BRAD BENDER!!"

The crescendo of screaming became harsh and metallic, and Brad awoke to the annoying buzz of his digital alarm clock. Six fifty-nine. He swatted it off, groaned, and stretched. Above him, through his bedroom's special skylight, he caught the deep blue of another June morning in southern California. He smiled and rolled on his side. Then he saw himself in the mirror, enough to thrill anyone. He had to admit it; those models in *GQ* had nothing on him. He smiled, lifted himself, and planted a kiss on his reflection. "You dog," he said, and winked.

His mother swung brightly through his bedroom door at 7:05 sharp, as he'd instructed her. The five minutes allowed him to sit up and think good thoughts about himself, to prepare his lap for the breakfast tray. "Good morning, sunshine," she said, smartly setting the orange juice and toast before him. She snapped a folded paper from under her arm and waved it at him. "You made All-State," she said.

"I always make All-State," he said.

His mother smiled benevolently. "Now hurry up and eat or you'll be late for school. Your father and Shelley have already left."

Brad looked down at the glass of freshly squeezed juice and the two slices of whole-grain bread. He sighed and shook his head. "Lightly toasted, Mom," he said. "*Lightly* toasted."

In the bathroom he whistled as he finished the last bit of stubble on his perfect square chin, and wiped off the remaining dabs of shaving cream. He flipped open the medicine cabinet and scanned the bottles and vials in alphabetical order—Brut, Clinique, Dior, on down to Ralph Lauren and Stetson. He chose Paco Rabane on the way back from Zetienne, splashed it on his face, and spun around in a move he'd been sharpening for prom night. He smiled at himself, widely, showing his perfect white teeth. His mother suddenly appeared in the mirror, holding out his letterman's jacket.

"Well," she said, "aren't we in an all-state mood?"

"They announce the Prom King today," he said.

"What's not to be happy about?"

"Bradley," his mother said. "I'm so proud of you. Who's going to be the lucky girl? Janet? Cindy? Sonya? Laura?"

Like a parrot, Brad recited, "Gloria? Becky? Juliette?" Then he slapped himself on the face, as if waking himself from a trance. "The possibilities are staggering." He was delighted to see Wylie Barrett appear behind his mother; Wylie was sort of a twerp, but he was funny and he did a wicked impersonation of Mrs. Bender. And he worshiped Brad. He stuck two fingers up behind Mrs. Bender's head and said, "Take Shirley Crater, guy."

Brad reacted as though he'd been socked in the solar plexus. Then he stuck his finger down his throat and made exaggerated gagging noises as he staggered to the toilet and pantomimed throwing up.

"Oh, Bradley, *really*," Mrs. Bender said. Wylie minced and mugged behind her, mouthing the words along with her. "Shirley's a *perfectly nice girl*."

"She's a bow-wow," Brad said. "Let Cliff Smert take her. *He's* an animal lover." He turned back to the mirror to finish his hair.

"So what about it, Chief," Wylie said. "Need a ride?"

"The scooter again, Wylie?" Brad said. His mother stood there with her arms crossed gazing at her son's reflection. Wylie nodded. "Thanks, sport. I'll take the Camaro." He turned around to face them and said, "Well? How do I look?"

"Aces," Wylie said, and his mother, so square, gave him thumbs-up.

●   ●   ●

Stan White, a hulking freshman who'd been recruited as Brad's personal bodyguard in September, had saved the parking spot right in front of the school by standing in it and threatening the life of anyone else who came close, and Brad calmly pulled the Camaro into the spot. He got out, nodded, and said, "Morning, Stan. You get the sports sections?"

"You bet," White said, and handed him the stack. Brad put them on the car's hood, signed them swiftly, and then began to saunter toward the school's front doors. He was suave, he was cool, he was definitely debonair. He was writing the book on charm. As if he were a magnet, girls began moving toward him, and he stopped to chat, flashing each one a smile, giving them a signed copy of the sports section with the All-State article. Then he saw Cliff Smert, scrubbed, pink-cheeked, dressed in a navy blazer and a rep tie, surrounded by a small crowd near the doors—Cliff, the president of the class, bound for Princeton, soon to be a registered Republican. What was he doing up there?

He felt a hand tighten around his arm and he turned to find Shirley Crater, the ugliest girl at Rockridge High. Who *cared* if she was a whiz at calculus? Who *cared* if her combined SATs were 1548? Her teeth were wrapped with shiny braces and the elaborate piece of orthodontic headgear she wore made her look like an alien. Her glasses had to be at least two inches thick, and her eyes, slightly crossed and magnified to the twelfth power, locked on his and burned with adolescent passion. It was like being adored by the Attack of the Crab Monsters. Her other claw now fastened around his sole remaining sports section. "Thanks," Shirley said in a husky voice.

Brad thought now he might *really* throw up. He
jerked the paper out of her hand in a spasm of instinct,
as one might get out of the way of a speeding car, as
Superman would recoil from Kryptonite, and began to
fumble his words, something he'd never done with a
football. "Gee . . . uh . . . sorry, Shirley . . . but I, uh
. . . already promised this last one to . . . uh . . . ." He
pulled away from Shirley, grabbed a passing freshman,
and jammed the paper into his arms. "Take it or die,"
Brad said under his breath.

Shirley Crater was sincerely disappointed. "Oh,
well," she said bravely. "When you get more." She
flashed him a huge metallic smile. "Bye," she said and
flounced off.

Only *he* could make the serious Shirley act like this.
He watched her go as if she were his life flashing before
him, and shuddered.

In homeroom, he lounged in the back with his cro-
nies, cracking gum and joking, while the principal, Mr.
Hiller, crooned the morning announcements. "So," he
said, "if you must chew gum between classes, swallow it
before re-entering.

"Now for the announcement you've all been waiting
for. The Senior Prom's Royal Court." Brad shushed his
buddies and sat up straight, waiting for the coronation.
"Last year the most popular girl chose her date, so this
year the most popular boy will choose. But *this* year
we're going to try something different. Something more
worthwhile than a popularity contest." Brad's grin
faded slightly and he swiveled his head, as if to hear better. Cliff Smert swung around in his chair and held up
something in one hand and a fistful of dollars in the

other. "To raise money for the library purchase program," Mr. Hiller continued, "we're going to have a lottery for a compact disc player, and whoever sells the most tickets in the next twenty-four hours will be this year's Rockridge High . . . "

So *that's* what that worm had been doing, Brad thought, as Cliff Smert shook the bills like a pompon. He was out the door before Mr. DeTaglia could stop him, and he burst into the principal's office just as Mr. Hiller finished the announcements.

Brad stood with his hands on his hips wondering what might happen to him if he strangled the principal. Detention, surely, maybe more. "How many?" the man said smugly. Brad grabbed the roll of tickets and pulled off about twenty, then handed the strip back to Hiller. "That oughtta cover it," he said and stalked out, slamming the door behind him.

Of all the boring subjects, science was the boringest, but Brad Bender wasn't bored today. He was thinking of ways to murder Cliff Smert. Mr. Rarrick, a short mousy man, was going on as passionately as ever. "Tonight's meteor shower is the largest of its kind in this hemisphere for as long as we've been keeping records, so it's a once-in-a-lifetime chance to get a bird's-eye view. I want you all to watch the meteor shower tonight, and I mean really *watch* it. Don't just take a glance out your window . . . "

Brad bent forward and crunched Smert's shoulder. "Think you're hot stuff because you got an hour jump on me, bozo?" he hissed. "Well, look at me. Do I look bothered to you? Do I look disturbed?"

"Seriously disturbed," Cliff said serenely.

"Yeah? Well, I eat twerps like you for breakfast and spit out the pencils," Brad said.

"Mr. Bender?" Mr. Rarrick said. "What's the assignment?"

Momentarily rattled, Brad said, "You asked us to, uh, take a shower." The class tittered.

"Meteors," Wylie said under his breath.

"You asked us to watch a meteor shower," Brad said.

"No, Mr. Bender," the geek said. "I *told* you to watch it."

"You're dogmeat, pal," Brad whispered to Cliff, but to tell the truth Cliff Smert didn't look terribly frightened.

Shirley Crater knew she wasn't beautiful and she knew she wasn't popular, but she *was* smart, and as soon as she got her braces off and talked her parents into contacts, and got *out* of southern California, she knew she'd be just fine. In the meantime she had this annoying and passionate crush on the handsomest, hunkiest boy in her class. Whenever she saw him, she felt woozy, really an uncomfortable feeling; but she knew that was what true love felt like. And from reading the Romantic poets, she knew she had to go for it or die.

As she walked out of the lunch line carrying her tray, she made straight for the table Brad Bender would sit at, the only empty table on the patio, guarded as always by that inscrutable muscular moron who'd signed on for a lifetime of humiliation in September. She eyed him carefully—he hadn't hit her yet—and put down her tray. "Hi, Stan," she said, trying to give her voice a lilt. She sat down. "This really *is* the best table—you're very smart to pick it. It's the nicest spot in the cafeteria, no wonder Brad sits here . . . "

"It's *taken*," Stan said.

"I know no one's supposed to sit here, except Brad, I mean, but I'm sure Brad won't mind; in fact we were talking just this morning and . . . I like your shirt. I mean, me and Brad have lots to talk about and I think it would be a very positive statement, I mean he's popular and I'm smart and if popular and intelligent people got together more often, do you know what I mean?" She was disheartened by the fact that today, like yesterday and the day before, Stan had picked up the chair with her in it and carried her to a table far away from Brad's. Today, however, she'd been lucky enough to grab her tray.

Brad set up shop at the table and made Stan monitor the line made up exclusively of girls willing to buy a ticket for the privilege of sitting, even momentarily, with him.

To Darcy Cook he said, "And the more tickets you buy, the more it clinches an already foregone conclusion—that you *will* be my choice for Queen."

To Debbie LaBrava he said, "Queen Debbie. I really like the sound of that. Sorta regal, know what I mean? How many did you say?"

To Marilyn Monrovia he said, "Perfect! *I'm* a Sagittarius too. So prom night's in the stars. Can I put you down for ten tick—"

To his horror he saw Shirley Crater on a collision course with his table. She'd taken off her glasses, changing her eyes from loony headlights to shriveled slits, and she hadn't gotten in line precisely because she couldn't see it. He quickly grabbed a freshman and swung him in front of her, like a tackling dummy. She walked right into him, and then she smiled brightly and grabbed his arm as she'd grabbed Brad's that morning, and she cooed, "I'll take ten. One at a time."

That night, after his favorite dinner, made by his mother, and the All-State eulogy, made by his father, Brad Bender retreated to his bedroom in order to gloat. When he had finished counting the ticket receipts, he put his feet up on his desk and dialed Cliff Smert.

"Hello, you have reached the Smert residence," Cliff said. "Cliff Junior speaking."

"How does the agony of defeat taste, you dork?" Brad said. "Like licking an ashtray?"

"You haven't won yet, Bender," Cliff said, but Brad could feel him squirming, even while the bravado ran on. He idly listened while he spun in his chair. Old Rarrick had been right; the sky was streaked with meteors. Pretty impressive, like all the touchdown passes he had caught. In fact, it looked like a cosmic tickertape parade. "Listen, Cliffy," he said. "The only thing that could stop me now is an act of God."

A roaring streak of light zipped past the skylight, so bright and loud that Bender was momentarily frozen. Then he ducked under his desk, dropping the phone. A white burst flashed moments later, accompanied by a tremendous explosion. He got to his feet, opened his window, and peered out, but everything looked normal. When he picked up the receiver, Cliff was saying over and over, "Brad? Brad? Are you all right?"

"You pray regularly, Smerty pants?" he said. And

then he shouted, "*Well, tell him he missed.*" He banged
down the receiver and turned toward the skylight again
just in time to see another meteor, bigger and brighter
than the previous one, headed right for his room. He
heard an accelerating noise, something between a rush
of wind and an approaching jet, and he dove under his
bed as the room exploded.

The scientists, newsmen, and police were there most
of the night. They came again in the morning, and Brad
was delighted with all the publicity. As the photog-
rapher from the Los Angeles *Times* made his way
around Brad's bedroom, Brad obliged by getting into as
many shots as possible. He was scheduled to appear on
the morning and evening news, and several radio news-
casts. There was even talk of a *National Geographic*
special. But the scientists, unfortunately, weren't interested in interviewing him at the moment; they were
far more fascinated by the bedroom itself. Brad decided
to stick around in case they had any more questions.

"This is incredible," one of the scientists said to him.
"I mean, practically everything in this room has been
magnetized. I'm surprised you're not." Brad smiled
politely and edged away from the man, who seemed a
little loony, like all scientists, back toward the full-
length mirror on his door. He nonchalantly glanced
over his shoulder to look at himself—he wouldn't want
to disappoint his fans—and what he saw made the blood
leave his brain. There was a metal ruler stuck to his
back, and his sweater looked like a desk blotter, covered
with paper clips.

"Have they located the other one?" another scientist
asked.

"No, they're still looking," the head guy said. "Personally, I have my doubts. The odds of two meteorites hitting on the same night are *astronomical*." They all laughed. It was the same dumb joke his dumb science teacher had made.

"I know, I know, but the whole neighborhood saw it. Even this young man . . . "

Brad hoped they wouldn't begin to question him; he didn't want to be interrupted from the difficult job of disengaging the ruler from his back. He turned slightly away from them and the arm of his desk lamp swiveled and bonged against his head, sticking fast. He laughed, a bit nervously. "Hey, you guys," he said, and then he remembered all the movies he'd seen. Scientists, once they discovered something weird, always took it apart in order to figure it out. He remembered *The Fly* and *The Thing* and *Iceman* and even *E.T.* He imagined himself strapped to a cold aluminum table, with one of those mercury vapor lights blaring into his eyes. A guy in a white lab coat with a Peter Lorre voice bent over him, saying, "We must measure this charge, young man, do not fear. The electrical flux. I'm just going to insert this tube into . . . "

All the scientists were looking at him, so he backed against the door and tried to smile as he said, "Pretty big hole, huh, guys?"

He locked the door the minute they left, but they hadn't been gone ten minutes when his mother called, "Brad-ley, come out of there. You're going to be late for skoo-ul."

"I'm not going," he said through the door.

"Why not?" she said. "Are you sick?"

"Yes," he said.

Then he heard Wylie's voice. "He's sick?"

"That's what he said," his mother said. "He's sick."

"What do you mean, you're sick?" Wylie said.

"I'm not going to school, Wylie," Brad said.

"Why not?" Wylie asked.

Brad looked at his reflection in the mirror. He'd been, well, picking things up, sort of. He was coated now with safety pins and straight pins, paper clips and staples, metallic paraphernalia he'd never even seen before. He didn't know where it had even come from, but it kept flying through the air and sticking to him.

"I can't tell you," he said, and his voice sounded horrible.

"You've *got* to go," Wylie said. "Either that or forfeit."

"I don't care about being King of the Prom," Brad said. The metal wastepaper basket skidded across the floor and stuck to his leg; he kicked it off.

"Or you forfeit to *Cliff*," Wylie said.

He sent Wylie on ahead and did his best to remove the assorted metallalia from his clothes, hair, and face. It was a sticky business; no sooner had he picked off a paper clip when he had to figure out a way to remove it from his hands. His charge was so strong it seemed to attract objects through cloth and leather; one look at his shoes told him that. He contented himself with prying stuff off with a plastic comb, almost like popping bottle tops.

But it wasn't until he got near the Camaro that he discovered the extent of his problem. He wrenched open

the door and lost his balance and fell when his hand
stuck tight. He unfastened it and tried to slam the door
but it flew back and smacked his arm. Trying to walk
away, he understood what Debbie LaBrava meant when
she'd told him, "I'm stuck on you."

Then even he saw the irony. *O Brad*, a million girls
sighed in unison, *you're so attractive*.

His anger building, he pried his hand off and gave the
door a good swift kick, but his shoe stuck to the side
and when he yanked it away, he again found himself on
his back. Furious, he got to his feet and looked for
something to bash the Camaro with, but the host of im-
plements hanging inside the garage door—a hoe, a
shovel, a pitchfork—would all be more trouble than
they were worth. Even as he watched, his sister's pink
bike detached itself from the garage wall, stood
straight, and began rolling toward him.

Stan White's face, usually impassive, registered shock
as Brad pulled into the parking spot Stan was holding
for him. "Not *one word*," Bender said. Trying to main-
tain a little dignity, he carefully swung one leg over the
bike, but he clattered to the pavement when the other
leg remained riveted to the pink bike's frame, and when
he looked up, White seemed embarrassed as he lay there
kicking at the bike.

It was do or die. He stood as best he could, dusted
himself off, and without another word marched past the
scores of double-takers toward Hiller's office. He'd
deposit the pouches of receipts and go home. But when
he announced his victory to Hiller, the principal said,
"Not so fast, Bradley. I must count the receipts," even

as his tie, held fast by his metallic tieclip, floated free from his jacket and pointed like a cobra at Brad Bender, that snake charmer.

So he waited around for the announcement, and things got worse, if that was possible. In science class, Rarrick rattled on, acting for the first time as though Brad Bender really were a celebrity. "The shower was spread over such a wide field," he said, "and the percentage of meteors that survive entry into the atmosphere is so small . . . Well, the odds against it happening to someone in our class . . . Mr. Bender?"

Brad sat miserably in his desk, feeling his shoes slithering backwards until they were attached to his chair's metal legs. The girl next to him wore large hoop earrings, and they looked like a magician's floating rings as they defied gravity by pointing to Brad. The girl who sat in front of him wore a necklace which had slid from her chest to her back and now rose into the air, straining toward him. When the braces on the fat kid next to him attached themselves to his arm, he stood up and excused himself, and as he stumbled out the door the waste paper basket rolled after him.

Classes were in session and the halls were deserted, so he thought he'd make a break for it while no one was watching. He started walking past the rows of lockers against the wall, heading for the door and home when he felt himself being pulled against his will, and the rubber soles of his shoes skidded across the linoleum as he tried to resist the magnetic pull. But not even he, All-State muscleman, had the strength. Soon he was spread-eagled against the lockers, stuck head to toe, his face mashed against a ventilation grille.

Close to tears, he gave himself up to the attraction

and tried to get his breath. Then he began to rock from side to side until he was able to flip over so his back was to the lockers, still stuck fast in a position of crucifixion, but at least no longer looking as though he was loving a wall of metal. In this position he tried to look relaxed as one of the sophomore math teachers, on her way to the Teachers' Lounge, passed. He gave her his most winning smile, and she nodded, a victory for Bender: she could have asked for his hall pass.

It took him most of the rest of the hour to work his way down the lockers, flipping from front to back, *bam! bam! bam!*, until, finally, he was able to wrench loose and fling himself with abandon against a cinderblock wall. He stood there, nonchalant as he could manage, while he watched a white-coated man standing in the door of Hiller's office. "It's quite unbelievable, of course," the man was saying, "but it seems there *were* two meteors, both falling in Rockridge, both hitting the bedrooms of students in this high school. We've got the other student under observation, but can you tell me where to find Brad Ben . . . "

So it was true: they were going to truss and roast him, stick him with prongs and wires and make him eat mercury. He'd be on a *National Geographic* special, but unconscious while they pointed to him with a rubber-tipped stick. He made a break for it while he still could, down the hall, around the corner—the delicate metallic hood on the water fountain called to him—and into that part of the school he knew best, the athletic wing. He knew lots of places to hide there.

He flung open the locker room door, and then stopped, his heart pounding, as he unstuck his hand from the doorknob. Trying not to make too much noise, he walked as carefully as he could down the center of the rows of lockers, hoping the dual attraction to left and right would leave him untouched. He was right, but as he walked, the locks themselves all stood up and saluted him.

But he'd been wrong; there was nowhere to hide. In the towel room, he saw another man in a white lab coat talking to old jowly Charlie, and Brad quickly ducked inside the equipment room and stood there in the dark, his back against the door, straining to hear what the men were saying. The darkness rustled, and then he felt a rounded mesh-like something attach itself to his leg. All around him the air was whining, vibrating. He switched on the light and stared in horror at the mistake he'd made. A catcher's mitt was stuck to his leg, and the whole room was loaded with row upon row of twitching javelins, cleated running shoes, their points sharp and silver in the fluorescent light, golf clubs, metal baseball bats. He had seconds, he could see, before the whole conglomerated weight of the athletic world joined forces against him. He managed to pull open the door and squeeze through it just as a huge clatter of objects hit the opposite side and fell to the floor.

He scooted past the scientist and Charlie. Their faces were grotesquely large and distorted as they said, "We'd like to talk to you, Mr. Bender . . . " He was running in slow motion, as if in a dream, as Mr. Hiller's voice came over the intercom.

"Your attention, please. The lottery tickets have been counted and this year's Prom King is BRAD BENDER!"

The bell rang and suddenly the halls were crowded with students, even as the air filled with metallic objects, pens and wire retainers, watches, earrings, jewelry of every cheap sort, flying at him until he was a slowly moving heap of metal. He was caught in air thick as chilled honey as people reached out to him, trying to grab hold.

But this time they were trying to attack. Girl after girl—Darcy Cook and Debbie LaBrava, Marilyn Monrovia and Janet, Cindy, Juliette, Laura—was screaming at him.

"Laura said she's going to be your date!" hissed Darcy.

"You jerk!" Debbie said.

"Did you tell Jeannie . . . ?"

"Liar . . . "

"You double-crossing bozo . . . "

He struggled past them all as best he could, fighting them off like opposing tacklers, even as more and more metal stuck to him—the janitor's mop bucket, a clipboard, several three-ring binders—and the rampaging scrap pile known as Bender clanged out the school's front doors followed by a rampaging mob.

He saw his sister's bike, his only hope of escape, and he headed for it. But he seemed to be making no progress: in fact he seem to be running backwards. And then he realized he was being pulled, slowly, inexorably, until he stuck with an enormous clong to the school flagpole. He realized he looked like a car accident. He found himself surrounded by the sadistic, curious, elongated nightmare faces of everyone he'd ever condescended to, or otherwise offended—geeky freshmen he'd undershorted, girls he'd put down, his teachers, all of them, snarling, screaming, yelling for vengeance.

"ALL RIGHT!" he screamed. "SO I'M MAG-

NETIC! SO WHAT!" He pried the catcher's mitt loose from his leg and flung it savagely into the crowd. It slid back and stuck against his shoe. "Big deal!"

But the crowd seemed to disagree. Now they stepped back and began to applaud his misfortune, to whistle and jeer and catcall. He looked around for a friend but there was no one he could count on. Was he hallucinating?

"So you thought my scooter wasn't good enough for you," Wylie snarled.

"*Lightly* toasted, you ungrateful brat?" his mother said.

"Never once did you offer to take out the garbage," his father yelled.

"You thought I liked guarding that parking space," Stan White said.

Was there no one who still loved and adored him? No one he could count on? Brad Bender heard a great clatter, as if a giant trash compactor was making its way toward him. It sounded like hundreds of pebbles rattling around in tin cans, like crowbars bashing car hoods, like all the beer cans made in Milwaukee being crushed. The crowd parted, like the Red Sea, and he saw another miracle. "Oh my GOD!" he screamed.

Coming toward him, borne on a tide of magnetism, covered as he was with metal—scrap metal, jewelry, kitchen utensils, foreign car parts—her rubber-soled Reeboks scratching against the sidewalk even as she was lifted out of herself by the inexorable force of her attraction to him, and with a look of complete abandon on her face, bliss incarnate, was Shirley Crater. The other meteor! he thought as she was swept closer, closer . . .

And then he felt himself unfasten from the flagpole. He grabbed backwards to hold on, but he too was being pulled, pulled toward Shirley. "Ah, God," he moaned. "Won't someone help me?" But the crowd was delirious with vengeance. His body leaned at a forty-five degree angle, his hands clawed the air. "Noooooo," he yelled as Shirley Crater, a hurtling projectile of surrender, her glasses now flung aside, her lips puckered, her eyes closed and her arms open, was flung against him. They kissed; he couldn't help it. Their metallic raiments smashed together, sending a small shower of scraps down among the heads of the ecstatic onlookers. Even Brad Bender had to admit the sheer force of their attraction.

GHOST TRAIN
by Steven Bauer

Based on the Universal Television series *Amazing Stories*

Created by Steven Spielberg

Adapted from the episode "Ghost Train"

Teleplay by Frank Deese

Story by Steven Spielberg

FENTON GLOBE KNEW ABOUT BEING HAUNTED BY THE past. When he'd married Joleen Sizemore and moved to Chicago, he was aware that his boyhood in Iowa, the rich black soil and rolling farmland, the miles and miles of corn, the herds of dairy cows, still held him tight. He was aware as well of the guilt he felt when he'd put his father in the nursing home after his mother died. He loved his father, and his son Brian was particularly devoted to the old man, but at the time the apartment they lived in was cramped and dark, and Fenton consoled himself by thinking that his father would rather look out the windows of a nursing home on cornfields than out the windows of his son's apartment on asphalt and automobiles.

And indeed Daniel Globe seemed just fine. The old man stared off into space a good deal, and occasionally his cracked blue eyes would narrow slightly, as if he heard something in the distance, the hoot of a train whistle or the barking of a dog. So even when Fenton and his wife and son moved to an airier, more spacious apartment, one with a guest room, he let his father stay put.

But by the age of forty-five, he knew it was time to go home—back to Iowa, back to an earlier sense of family. He wasn't going to rise to the top in the insurance business, and when he was honest with himself, he knew he didn't care. So he bought the parcel of land in Janesville near where he'd grown up, and built the house he and Joleen had always wanted. They wouldn't have much money now—he'd taken a job as an agent with a small insurance firm near Waterloo—but they had a new house, they were in Iowa, and they all would be together. Maybe they'd get a horse if they could afford to fence the place, and he'd have a small garden. He'd get dirt under his fingernails. Everything was going to be swell.

When Fenton and Joleen went to get his father, the manager of the Shady Nook Nursing Home told him the old man had been acting strangely ever since being told about the move. "The other day we found him wrapping Christmas presents," Mr. Cole said. It was the middle of August. "I've also heard some of our other residents talking about how old Mr. Globe is planning to go on a long trip, one he's been waiting for all his life."

"Sounds like Dad's telling tales again," Fenton said. "When I was a boy he told the most amazing stories."

"Maybe so," Mr. Cole said. "Still, it's not uncommon for folks his age to start having delusional fantasies."

"My father's mind is as sound as a steel bridge," Fenton said. "Always has been."

• • •

The ride along Interstate 80 wasn't much fun—semis and diesel smoke and exhaust. But Fenton turned off at Malcolm and took State Route 63 north, over the Iowa River, toward Tama and Toledo, a few miles east of the Mesquakie Indian Settlement. Soon the air was heavy with the hot, late summer smells of alfalfa, corn, and cows. His father, like a kid, was standing with his head stuck out the Chrysler's sunroof.

"How's it smell up there?" Fenton yelled to his father.

"Fine," the old man said. "Just fine." He sat down and started playing with the toggle switch on the station wagon's back door, raising and lowering the electric window.

"I think you'll love the new house, Dad," Fenton said. "I designed it myself with a bedroom on the ground floor for you so you won't get tired going up and down stairs."

"Nothing the matter with me," the old man said.

"And Fenton had them put a special heater in your room so you won't get cold at night."

"That's mighty thoughtful, but I won't be around long enough to enjoy it."

"Don't go talking like that, Dad. People can convince themselves of anything. You said yourself there's nothing wrong with you. You've got years and years ahead."

"You said the house is near Waterloo?" his father asked.

"That's right," Fenton said. "In Janesville. I think you'll recognize the area. It's not that far from the home place."

"Just a cornfield, you said? Funny you taking me to where I should of died seventy-five years ago."

"Now Dad," Fenton said. "It's one thing fooling with your friends at Shady Nook, but if you go talking like that to Brian, he'll never get to sleep. You know what an imagination he has."

"He can't wait to see you, Opa," Joleen said. It was the name Brian had coined for his grandfather, a derivative of *grandpa* by way of *old pa*.

"Maybe someday soon you could take me out to where it happened," the old man said. "I ain't been out there since you put me in that place."

"Won't have to drive far," Fenton said. "Turns out the rails used to run right through the field behind the house. I own it."

"Your property?" Daniel said. "The accident happened on your property?"

"Yeah," Fenton said. "Can you beat that? Didn't even know until after I closed. The old gal at the deed office in Waterloo told me."

"Exactly where on your property?" Daniel asked.

As they turned off the dirt road and drove up the newly paved driveway, Fenton was struck once again by how disconcertingly odd the house looked out here. It was spanking new, dazzlingly white with its aluminum siding glaring in the August sun, two stories, three bedrooms, a TV room and family room and big eat-in kitchen. A two-car garage. Shutters on all the windows. Around it, the land spread as it had for hundreds of years. Only the house was new.

He shook his head slightly, as though that might dislodge the thought. Brian came running from behind

the house yelling, "Opa! Opa!" His father was out of
the car in an instant. He gathered Brian up and swung
him around until the boy clung piggyback to the old
man's shoulders. He was delighted by the bond between
them and now wished he'd gotten to this sooner.

"Brian, be careful," Joleen said, but Daniel just
shook his head at her to tell her it was all right. Fenton
watched his father closely as the old man stared at the
house. He was surprised by how old his father looked in
the pitiless light. His hair was white; his eyes seemed to
have sunken in his skull, so even in the stark sun
darkness pooled around them. His beard was white and
scrawny, and his face looked gaunt and long, as though
gravity, working on him for three quarters of a century,
had stretched the flesh.

"So what do you think, Dad?" Fenton asked.

"I don't like it," his father said. "No, sir. Not a bit."

"Maybe you'll like it better from inside," Joleen
said.

"Oh, the *house* is fine," Daniel said. "It's mighty big
and fine. I don't like where you put it is all."

Daniel Globe hid the carefully wrapped Christmas
presents on a closet shelf and went back to his suitcase.
No, he thought. Where his son had put the house was a
big mistake. He snapped the clasps and stared down
at his old clothes, slightly musty from the laundry at
the Shady Nook. Fenton had gone to all this trouble,
strictly unnecessary. Daniel Globe didn't expect to be
around long enough to appreciate it.

He knew the train would come. He pulled out all the
clothes and checked to make sure his ticket was still
where he'd put it. Then he made his way toward the

kitchen, all linoleum and formica and glittering stainless steel, not at all like his Maisie's kitchen, dark with wood and age.

"Don't make me say it again," Joleen scolded. "Your grandpa is ten times older than you so he needs ten times the rest."

"But I only want to ask him about the Indians," Brian said. "He doesn't have to run or nothing."

"Maybe tomorrow."

"But I never get to play with anyone," Brian said. "None of the kids at school come 'cause it's too far on their bikes." Daniel stuck his head around the corner, catching Brian's attention. He put his finger to his lips and made sure Joleen hadn't seen him.

"You have plenty of toys to play with," Joleen said.

"Okay," Brian said, running out of the kitchen. Joleen watched him go in amazement. When she turned her back, Daniel hurried past and out the door into the sunlight.

The grass and foxtails were knee-high on him as he walked, holding his grandson's hand, his eyes intent on the ground.

"Is this where the Indians used to fight, Opa?" Brian asked.

"It's one of the places," Daniel said.

"Which Indians was it?"

"Right around here the Sac chief Keokuk fought off the Sioux," he said.

"Did you ever know anyone that was scalped by an Indian?" Brian asked.

"Brian, the Indians were the first people on this land," Daniel said. "It was theirs, all of it. You ask me,

they had a right to do what they had to do to protect
their families and land and way of life.''

Brian tugged his hand away, stooped, and picked
something up. "Look, Opa! It's an arrowhead. I found
a Indian arrowhead.''

Daniel took the object from Brian and studied it. As a
boy, he'd found dozens of artifacts in the fields around
the homestead. But this one was just a sharp rock.
"Sorry, boy,'' he said.

But something else caught his eye. Now he stooped
and picked up the rusty piece of iron about a half-foot
long.

"Wow,'' Brian said. "Is that a Indian spear?''

Daniel laughed and said, "No, Brian. It's a railroad
spike.''

"From a train?'' Brain asked. "You mean a real train
used to come through here?''

Daniel nodded, intent on studying the ground for
more evidence. "The Highball Express,'' he said,
"came right through here where we're walking.''

"Which way did it go?'' Brian asked.

"That's what we're gonna find out,'' Daniel said.

He kept walking. A hundred yards later, he found a
twisted, rusted piece of an ancient semaphore in the
weeds, and beyond that three railroad ties, still in position, though the tracks themselves had been removed.

He'd been about Brian's age, maybe just a touch
younger. There'd been no crops at all; it was grazing
land then; and there'd been a stand of trees over there,
he thought, where that blue water tower was.

"What happened here?'' Brian asked. He held a piece
of torn metal in his hands.

"The old Highball Express ran clear off its tracks.

Killed everyone on board.''

''You see it?'' Brian asked. Daniel nodded, knelt, and put his ear to the ground where the rail once had been. He saw something through the weeds, something glaringly white.

''It went straight west to east not veering an inch,'' Daniel said. He knelt and pointed due west.

''Bam!'' Brian said. ''Right through our new house.''

His son thought he'd been getting progressively stranger, Daniel knew, and of course he had, staring out across the cornfield, taking walks late at night, lying with his ear to the ground even right after a rain. He spent most of his time with Brian, and this evening especially it was important. There were things he needed to explain to this boy who played so intently with his toy train. As the small-gauge locomotive pulled its load of boxcars and passenger cars around the figure-eight layout, Brian maneuvered a dump truck into position on the tracks and Daniel winced as the locomotive hit the truck, buckled, lifted from the rails, and turned on its side.

Brian stared at him for a few seconds and then said, ''Opa? What made the Highball Express go off its track?''

If he didn't tell the boy tonight, he never would.

''Some little boy,'' he said, ''about your age, was waiting for the number 407 to pick him up and take him to visit his grandpa in Sioux City. The train was running late, and the boy got tired and bored, so he lay down near the track with his ear to the rail so he could hear if the train was coming.''

''Like you sometimes lie in the field?'' Brian asked.

"Yes," Daniel said. "The boy got very tired, because he fell asleep right there. I've never understood this part, but when the train came—hooting its whistle and rumbling and clanging—he didn't wake up. The brake-man saw him suddenly, I guess, and he threw the brake hard, locking the wheels on the Highball Express. And all that weight and pressure just made the track turn on itself." Brian's eyes were very big. "And that little boy woke just in time to see the whole train lift up and roll over like a trained dog. Just in time to hear the screams of the passengers." He took a handkerchief from his pocket and wiped his eyes.

Brian's voice was hushed. "Were you that little boy, Opa?"

"I *am* that little boy, Brian, and tonight that old 407 is going to do what it shoulda done seventy-five years ago. It's going to take me where I ought to be."

"How long will you be gone?" Brian asked.

"Boy, I'm never coming back." Brian's face had grown white; he'd scared the kid. "Well," he said, clapping his hands and getting to his feet, "come on, boy, we got work to do. That train should just miss your parents room when it comes through the house. But you and me, we're right in the way. We got to get some stuff moved."

"That's enough," Fenton said, suddenly appearing in the doorway.

"You been spying on me?" Daniel said, his voice low and harsh. "You let me be."

"If you're living here, Dad, you've got to follow house rules and number one is not telling scary stories to Brian. You know how susceptible he is."

"I've been telling you and telling you, but you just

won't listen. You better start packing some stuff, and get yourselves somewheres else to sleep."

Fenton's face was very red and his hands were now tight on his hips. "You've gone too far today, Dad. I'm sorry." He turned and left the room.

"Come here, boy," Daniel said, reaching out and grabbing Brian by the sleeve. "Around midnight you'll be seeing a yellow light like you never saw before, coming in this house from the eye of an iron dragon. Then you'll smell wood burning though it's only early September, and you won't know where it's coming from. And you'll hear a long mournful whistle warning you to get out of the way."

"What're we going to do?" Brian asked, hunching his shoulders.

"I suppose the only thing we *can* do, seeing your pa don't believe me, is to get a few of your favorite things to where they'll be safe." He looked around the room at Brian's toys and mementos, some G.I. Joe dolls, a gray plastic Transformer, an autographed baseball, a Chicago Cubs pennant, an old stuffed elephant. "If you wanted to save something in here, what would be first?"

Brian ran to him and he held out his arms. Into the muffle of shirt where Brian stuffed his face the boy said, "You, Opa. I'd save you first."

Fenton and Joleen were in the kitchen. "I think they've finally gone to bed," he said. "For a while there, I was sure I'd have to call that doctor. You know, all his life he's been unable to forget or live down that accident."

"Who could?" Joleen asked. "It's a hideous thing to live with."

"But he never talked about it much before," Fenton

said. "It was always left untalked about."

"That's the way it was with my Grandpa Noble. He never once talked about the fleet he'd steered into German waters until he went nuts and told everyone that same fleet had docked in Lake Michigan to give him another chance."

Fenton looked sharply at his wife. "It's not the same."

"What is it then?"

"I think it's the move," Fenton said. "Being back where he grew up." There was a loud bang and a shriek of laughter from the stairway to the second story. Fenton sat up straight. Then a series of thuds. "What the hell is going on?" Fenton yelled as he stalked from the kitchen into the living room.

Brian had been trying to help his grandfather carry a trunk, but he'd let it go and the old man was pulling on it as it bumped from stair to stair. He stopped for a minute and looked up at Fenton. "Don't worry, son," Daniel Globe said. "The way I got it measured the Highball'll miss your room completely and only take out half the kitchen. But Brian and me, hell, we're right in the way. You two run along to bed; we'll fend for ourselves."

"Dad," Fenton said. "If you're so sure about all this, why don't you show me where the tracks are."

"Don't be stupid," his father said. "They tore out those tracks years ago."

"Then how can a train pass through this house if it isn't on tracks?"

"The Highball Express don't need no tracks just as a ghost don't need wings and a propeller to fly."

Fenton looked at his wife who was making circles

around her right ear with her index finger. He'd better be calling that doctor after all, he thought.

Fenton met Dr. Steele at the front door when he arrived and filled in the sketchy details he'd given over the phone. So Dr. Steele was able to say, when Fenton took him to the room where the old man was folding and refolding his clothes, "Mr. Globe, I've come to talk to you about a train called the Highball Express."

"Well, it's about time," Daniel said. "I've been trying to tell these people all day now, but they won't listen to me. Maybe you can talk a little sense into them. Now I know we don't have time to move the house, but if we could just take out some of the valuables, it might help when the insurance guy arrives tomorrow."

"What makes you so sure it's coming tonight?" the doctor asked, his hands inside his black bag. Fenton could see he was preparing a syringe.

"Because I did what I used to do all the time as a boy," his father said. "I put my ear to the track and heard it."

"And it's going to stop for you?"

"I know it is. I've got a ticket." He reached into his pocket and fumbled for the piece of paper stuck there. Fenton held him by the shoulders while the doctor swabbed the interior of his elbow with a cotton swab.

"What are you doing to Opa?" Brian asked.

"Here's my ticket," Daniel said. "You want to see it, boy?" He handed it to Brian. He seemed not to have noticed the hands holding him or the needle until it was already in his arm. "Ouch!" he said. "What was that? A danged yellow jacket?"

"Just something to help you sleep before your trip," the doctor said.

"But I can't fall asleep," the old man said. "That's what happened the last time. That was the whole problem. That's why all those people died, don't you see?"

"No one blames you, Dad," Fenton said. "You're making a fool of yourself. It was an accident."

"No," the old man said, beginning to stagger. "This isn't right. It can't be like this."

"Relax, Mr. Globe," the doctor said. "We won't let you miss your train." Fenton was holding his father now, as he grew heavier by the second. With the doctor's help, he half carried, half dragged the old man into the first floor room he'd made for him, and laid him on the bed.

"No," Brian said. "Don't you see?" His mother was gently shaking him as tears ran down his cheeks. "He missed the train the first time because he was sleeping. That's why it's coming back. He can't sleep in there. The train goes right through that room. It'll run him over."

His mother held him at arm's length and looked at him seriously, the way she always did when she wanted him to listen. "Look at me, Brian. Do you really think your father would put Opa somewhere he could get hurt?"

"I don't know," Brian said.

"Would he, Brian?" his mother persisted.

"No, but . . ."

"No, he wouldn't," his mother said. "Now you get up to bed like a good boy, okay?"

Grownups never understood. Clutching the ticket to the Highball Express, Brian ran upstairs to his room.

Once inside, he closed the door firmly and made sure it stuck. He turned on a light and studied the ticket, yellow and crinkled, dated 1910. He still didn't know for sure if the train was coming tonight, but that's what Opa had said, and he believed everything Opa told him.

He walked to his bulletin board and, using a straight pin, fastened the ticket to the cork. He turned back the covers on his bed, hunched on the mattress, and opened the window. The moon was almost full and the night was clear, but as far as he could see, he saw only moonlit grasses and weeds, no sign of the Highball Express. Off in the distance, a dog barked.

He jumped from bed, turned off the light, and set up his telescope on its tripod, but when he peered through the eyepiece, he still saw nothing. For a moment he was seduced by the stars themselves, the night sky brilliant here as it had never been in Chicago. But it wasn't the stars tonight he should be watching for. It was the Highball Express. He got off the bed, down on his knees, and put his ear to the floor. He squinted as if to listen harder, but still he heard nothing. He closed his eyes.

It was about midnight when he awoke. The wind had picked up considerably and a few loose papers flew around on the floor. Through the white eyelets of his curtains a yellow light shone, casting a varying weaving pattern across his ceiling and walls. Not too far in the distance, a long, drawn-out, lonesome wail sounded, the drone of an airhorn. He rubbed his eyes with his fists and turned on his side. But the airhorn brought him wide awake as he realized he wasn't dreaming. He swung into a kneeling position, knocking over the telescope, and, scrambling onto his bed, he stared out the window. The wind flattened his hair and ruffled his pajamas. In the moonlight, he saw the long, dim silhouette of a train, and at its head a locomotive with a huge yellow eye, heading straight for the house.

He was out of his room in a second, beating on his parents' door with his fist, yelling, "Mom! Dad! It's coming. It's coming fast."

"Brian?" He could hear his mother's drowsy voice. "You have a nightmare?"

"The train! I saw it. The Highball Express. It's coming right at us. Hurry."

"Brian, be quiet. You'll wake your grandfather," his father said.

With a shock he remembered why it was coming, and he whispered "Opa" even as he ran back into his room and grabbed the train ticket from the cork board where he'd pinned it. He flew down the shaking stairs; the night was filled with a dense rumble, coming from the ground beneath the house, and the engine's huge yellow searchlight seemed to fill the downstairs. The airhorn sounded again.

Brian banged open his grandfather's door. Opa lay on his back, his mouth open, his arm hooked backwards over his forehead. "Opa," Brian yelled. "Hurry!" He was sitting on the old man's waist now, pulling on his shirt, shaking him. "Opa! You got to get up. It's the Highball Express. It's here. It's coming through your room."

The old man stirred, and his eyes blinked open. "What?" he said. "The 407?"

Brian could hear his father yelling as he came down the stairs, and then over his shoulder he saw his mother standing dazed in the doorway of his grandfather's room. "Mom," Brian yelled. "Hurry." But she turned back to his father.

Without waiting a second longer, Brian dragged his grandfather by the armpits off the bed and toward the door. The old man was coming fully awake now and stumbled to his feet, hurrying along with Brian.

They'd gotten behind a couch. The entire house was shaking on its foundation, as if a tornado swirled around it. The downstairs air was violently yellow, and the boy's ears were screaming with the sound of the train's whistle and horn. And then the front wall of the house exploded.

Plasterboard, wood struts, glass, and cement flew violently inward. Brian saw the front door come unhinged and wheel across the room like a skidding automobile. His mother's breakfront split down the middle and fell to the floor. The noise was horrible, a rending, tearing, screeching crash.

In the living room, coming to a halt, was an eighteen-ton locomotive, black as coal, steam gushing from its wheels. It slid to a stop now on invisible rails. From the windows of the passenger cars an eerie light glowed, mixing with the yellow eye of the locomotive to bathe the house in sickly bruising colors. There were people on the train who now peered out at Brian and his family; the women wore black felt hats decorated with pheasant feathers, their faces obscured by black net veils; the men's suits had wide lapels, and almost all of them wore vests. Brian had never seen clothes like those before, except in a book at school.

The conductor was trying to pull down a set of collapsible stairs. "Dang this thing," he said. "Never works, never works." He saw Brian's mother huddled in her bathrobe, and he tipped his hat and said, "Evening, ma'am." Then in his most authoritarian voice he yelled, "All aboard. Have your tickets ready, please."

At his side, his grandfather stiffened. "My ticket," he said. "Can't go without my ticket."

"Here's your ticket, Opa," Brian said, and handed it to him. "Can I come too?"

His grandfather kneeled and touched his chin; his eyes were kind, a little sad, and very young, like the eyes of a nine-year-old boy. "I'm sorry, Brian. You belong here with your mom and dad. And I belong on that train."

"You going to see *your* grandpa in Sioux City?"

"Well, boy," Opa said. "It's not quite that easy."

"But you'll be back in a little while, won't you?"

"I'm afraid not this time," his grandfather said. "But you'll be fine, I know you will."

"Who's gonna tell me stories about where the Indians fought and all that stuff?"

"You remember what I already told you? About the trading posts and war parties and the Pony Express? As long as you remember those, I'll always be here with you."

"Are you ready, Mr. Globe?" the conductor said.

"I hope my ticket is still good," Opa said, and handed the man the crumpled yellow paper.

"Always was, Mr. Globe. We've been waiting a long time for it."

Now his grandfather turned to his mother and said, "Thanks for taking me in, Joleen. Sorry I couldn't stay longer."

"All aboard!" the conductor yelled.

The old man hugged his son, gave Joleen a kiss on the cheek, and then came back to where Brian stood. He stooped down and shook Brian's hand. "And your dad thought I was losing my marbles," he said. "I've got a mind like a steel trap," he said. "Always have. Your Christmas present is in the closet in my room." He pushed something into Brian's hand.

The faces of the passengers on board were wreathed with smiles as they saw the old man board, and barely was he up those stairs when the conductor flipped them, jumped onto the platform, and the train began to move, slowly at first, its pistons churning against the wheels, steam billowing, and then with greater and greater speed as the huge black iron wheels turned faster and faster.

In no time at all, it seemed, they were alone. Brian's father huddled with his arm around Brian's mother, and the boy stood by himself, staring out the huge hole in the house through which the train had passed. And then it seemed to mend itself slowly at first and then with greater and greater speed, until the living room was itself again, plasterboard and wood, glass and cement, untouched. He wheeled and ran into the room where his grandfather had lain, but there was no one there, just the imprint of an old frail body on the bed. He ran back into the living room where his parents still stood. He flung open the front door and ran outside.

The night was quiet and lit by the moon. The tall grass and weeds receded into the distance, tipped as with frost by the silver light. Off to the west, he saw a small

yellow spot, like a firefly or a star, moving at incredible
speed, and he heard the long mournful wail of an
airhorn, the clatter and crash of horses, and the wild
windy yells and whoops of what might have been, he
thought, a Sioux war party. He looked down at the
palm of his hand where an arrowhead lay.

THE SITTER
by Steven Bauer

Based on the Universal Television series *Amazing Stories*
Created by Steven Spielberg
Adapted from the episode ''The Sitter''
Teleplay by Mick Garris
Story by Joshua Brand and John Falsey

WHEN I WAS SEVEN AND MY BROTHER EIGHT, MY parents were divorced, and we moved from Malibu to the San Fernando Valley. We'd been a pretty happy family, or so Lance and I had thought; my father made good money as an advertising executive, all the better to buy us the latest high-tech toys, and my mother had quit her job selling real estate in order to stay home with us, her big mistake, to fulfill our every whim.

We were spoiled and unruly children, used to getting our own way, and when my mother left my father, we blamed the disruption of our lives on her. We missed the beach and the sunsets and all our friends. We didn't think for a minute about what she missed or had given up, and when she had to go back to work full-time, we didn't lose a minute letting her know how much we resented the new shape our lives had taken.

My mother and Lance and I took possession of our new house—a tacky two-bedroom ranch in a run-down subdivision called Rancho Estates—on a sultry, smoggy day in July. The moving men dripped with sweat, and my mother's blonde hair curled in tendrils from the humidity. Gamely, she hustled in and out of the house, carrying boxes, delivering glasses of instant iced tea, trying to speak brightly to the two white and two black men who were sullen and silent as they lugged my mother's share of the furniture into the house. Did we help? Only slightly, mainly to let the men know where the boxes marked TOYS were to go. When they finally left, our microwaved dinners got cold as we searched the KITCHEN boxes for silverware.

I wore thick glasses then, and I had a cowlick, which made me the perfect little twerp, and Lance had a bully's sneer and freckles and the wide opaque eyes of a young criminal. We'd already decided not to give the place a chance, had begun our guerrilla war to let our mother know how unhappy we were.

"I hate Sun Valley," I said. "It makes my eyes sting."

"There aren't any kids in the neighborhood," Lance said.

"I can't breathe," I said, "there's so much smog."

"Yeah," Lance said, "the ocean air was better. Dad says—"

My mother interrupted the litany. "You'll grow to love it here," she said. "I promise. Just give it a little time. Maybe you can find somebody who has a pool."

"In Sun Valley?" Lance said. "Probably nobody here even has a bucket."

"It's too hot," I said. "Why couldn't we get a house with air conditioning? Dad's house has air conditioning."

"This food stinks," Lance said. "Dad always takes us out to eat."

That did it, as we both knew it would. Like most

adults, my mother was susceptible to guilt, and we could almost always, as we just had, reduce her to tears.

In the morning, we started in again, Lance racing from room to room firing his phaser gun, which made a noise like the dying whine and bam of very good fireworks. My mother stalked the house looking for her attaché case, unaware that I was sitting quietly applying watercolors to its patent leather exterior. Cartoons blared from the television, so loud they could be heard all over the house. "Did either of you kids see my briefcase?" my mother yelled. As usual, we ignored her. "Earth to Lance and Dennis," she said. Lance was standing on the couch now, firing at me, adding his screams to the gun's shrieks. "Stop that, Lance," Mom said, and then saw what I was doing. "Damnit, Dennis," she said and wrenched the briefcase away.

"Don't you like it?" I asked.

The doorbell rang. "That must be the sitter," my mom said, and as she hurried off, Lance looked at me, and I looked at him, and we grinned. The real fun was about to begin.

Her name was Patti, and she drove a red Mustang; she was seventeen and she wore her long blonde hair in a ponytail that reached beyond the small of her back. "Don't give Patti a hard time," my mother admonished.

"Oh, don't worry, Mrs. Paxton," Patti said. "I get along real well with kids."

"That's nice, dear," my mom said, relieved to be rid of us for eight hours. "Call me if you need me."

Patti needed her, all right, but she didn't call; in fact,

she ran right past our mother, screaming, as Mom pulled into the driveway. She was holding the blunt edge of hair sticking out from the rubber band where we'd cut off the ponytail. When my mother opened the door, we screeched to a halt, our faces smeared with warpaint (eyeshadow and lipstick), and Lance stopped whipping his imaginary horse with a lash made of the hair of a paleface woman we'd kidnaped and tortured.

Mrs. Abbott was next. "You kids remember our bargain," my mother said. "You give Mrs. Abbott any trouble and no Magic Kingdom. Understand?" We smiled demurely. Mrs. Abbott was perfect: a widow in her sixties, she had the square-faced, cold-eyed, no-nonsense look that was an invitation to mayhem. She was brash and forthright, wore a cardigan sweater in that heat, and carried a knitting bag under one arm and a tiny dustmop of a dog under the other. "I should tell you," my mother confided, "the boys get a little rambunctious now and then."

"Oh, I know all about little boys," said Mrs. Abbott, the little old lady who lived in a shoe. "Rambunctious is what they're all about. Mr. Abbott, God rest his soul, was an amateur prizefighter and he taught me a few of his tricks. So if the fellas here give me any guff, Mr. Weege here and me will knock them into the middle of next week. Isn't that right, Mr. Weege?" She squeezed the dog with her elbow and he yelped, as though someone had sat on a whoopee cushion.

We were good until after lunch. She sat in a chair knitting, watching *As the World Turns,* when Lance changed the channel to cartoons.

"Put that back!" Mrs. Abbott said. Her tone

brought Mr. Weege to a state of semi-wakefulness, and he squeaked loudly.

"We want to watch cartoons," Lance said.

"I want to see my soap," the old woman said, "and when I'm in your house I make the rules. Why don't you go out and get some fresh air?"

I reached across her knitting and patted Mr. Weege where I thought his eyes must be. "He's a cute puppy," I said adorably.

She was instantly mine. "Isn't he a pretty boy," she said.

Lance and I had a kind of perverse ESP those days. "There's a little puppy next door who'd love Mr. Weege," he said. "Can we bring him over to play?"

We'd just met Cupcake, a full-grown Doberman, the day before, and we managed to drag him into our house without getting bitten. He chased Mrs. Abbott in figure eights, Mr. Weege so terrified he gave off a palpable air of breathless astonishment until we were sure we could see his bugged-out little eyes. It ended with Mrs. Abbott screeching from the sofa as we got Cupcake to leave by tossing the hamburger my mother had defrosted for dinner out the back door. Then we made her the Choco-Lax cocoa to calm her frazzled nerves. The ambulance had arrived to carry her off, badly shaken and quite dehydrated, just as my mother was getting home from work.

Had a child psychologist been brought in, he might have twirled his pencil and spoken of broken families, childish insecurities, repressed hostility, and boredom. Had he been smart he also would have spoken of downright meanness. Lance and I needed a dose of heavy medicine, from a special kind of doctor.

• • •

As might be expected, word of the Paxton fiends got around, and my mother's list of babysitters grew thick with crossed-out possibilities. She became wily on the phone, attempting to secure a promise before revealing her name, or even our address after she tried giving an alias. Usually the mention of "Mrs. Paxton" caused the person being called to hang up unceremoniously.

We'd just about plucked my mother's last frail nerve when she found an ad for the Happy Helper agency and gave them a call. "Hello," she said. "I need a babysitter for my two little boys. Seven and eight." She paused. "Mrs. Paxton," she said. And then in a voice of utter disbelief, "You *can*? That's fantastic! Here's the address . . ."

We were busy setting up the bucket of cold water over the door to our room when Jennifer Mowbray arrived.

How to describe her? A black-skinned Carmen Miranda, a caricature of a caricature, a miracle. She was big, with a chest so large it looked like a huge pillow, and ample hips which made her swivel instead of walk. She wore a widebrimmed loosely woven straw hat and her dress that first day was flimsy cotton, a riot of parrots and palm trees and bougainvillea. She had a hardly believable smile and teeth like a croc's, eyes perpetually wide open in homage to the world's wonders, a gold hoop through her right earlobe, and chains of cheap beads around her neck. Her voice had the lilting rhythms of Jamaica, the racing highs and lows of inflection which made her sound part quizzical, part peremptory. She smoked a thin dark cheroot.

The door swung open on this vision, this perfect victim, and she said, "Hello, little missy. I am Jennifer. The agency sent me."

My mother was as surprised as I was; no one in Sun Valley looked like Jennifer—no one in Malibu either. Jennifer was from TV shows, or books, from another world entirely. "Oh, I'm glad to see you, Jennifer," my mother said, and ushered her inside. Lance went tiptoeing by, a coil of rope in his hand, like a character from a Warner Brothers cartoon. My mother missed him in her discombobulation, but Jennifer didn't.

"Look," my poor mother said. "These boys are a little on the rambunctious side, I ought to warn you. Boys, come here and meet Jennifer."

But Jennifer waved her hand in the air as if warding off gnats. "Oh, they just being boys," she said. "They got the imaginaries, is all. They just need to occupy their noodles is all they need. They just doing boys' stuff, missy. You run along to work and I'll find the little fellows okay."

We didn't need finding; we were hiding behind the door to our room, peeking out the crack at the two of them. Lance had fixed the piece of wood, and the rope, and the bucket, and when Jennifer found us, her wide-brimmed hat was in for an early morning rainstorm. My mother shrugged and went out the door, and we listened impatiently to the sound of Jennifer humming in the living room. And then we heard the heavy sound of her footsteps coming toward us.

Lance couldn't wait. "Jennifer," he called. "We're in here." We ran to the opposite wall, the better to see the whole panorama, just as Jennifer flung open the

door and strode into the doorway, stopping directly
under the bucket of water. Everything worked like a
charm—the wood slipped, the bucket tilted, the water
poured. But Jennifer must have had a charm of her own
because the water froze in midair, as though time had
stopped in that one small corner of the universe, while it
went on everywhere else. "Hello, little gentlemens,"
Jennifer said. "I be in the kitchen if you need me." And
she was gone.

Lance and I raced over to the doorway and looked up
in awe at the frozen cascade which promptly unfroze
now that Jennifer was gone and soaked us both to the
skin. We heard her voice lilting like water. "You little
mens like to play little games, don't you?" she said.
"Oh, I like games. It's just hard for little boys to fool
old Jennifer. Jokes on old Jennifer sometime loop-the-
loop." And then she laughed.

She came into the bedroom while we were changing
clothes, and we made her turn her back until we were
done. "You little mens better watch out for the colds,"
she said. "You give Jennifer them wet clothes."

"You talk funny," I said, watching her closely.

"Yeah," Lance said. "Where're you from?"

"Oh," she said, "I am from a very far-away place in
the Islands."

"Like Hawaii?" Lance asked.

"Somethin' like dat," she said, and the look in her
eyes became very far-away. She stood and swayed as she
spoke, as if moved by forces we couldn't see. "A special
place, with magic in the winds. The good wind come on
shore in the morning, and the bad wind blow out the

darkness. Everybody be happy and dancing and singing, a place little mens like yous would love to see."

"There's no place like that," Lance said indignantly. "Just in books."

"Little mens like you gots lots to learn 'bout the world past your back door. 'Specially in Sun Valley."

But I wasn't much interested in geography just then. I was more involved in paying Jennifer back. "Let's play hide and seek," I said, and Lance said, "Yeah!" This was an old routine of ours, and we had it down pat.

Jennifer looked puzzled. "I don't know dat play ting," she said.

"It's easy," Lance said. "You hide and we try and find you. We close our eyes and count to fifty to give you time to get away."

"You little crocodiles aren't going to be playing some fun on old Jennifer?" She blew a thin stream of smoke from her cheroot into the air, then stubbed it out in a little silver case she had strapped to her belt.

"Are you kidding?" I said. "We *always* play hide and seek with our sitters." We didn't give her a chance to say a word; we turned our backs, covered our eyes, and loudly began counting.

She tiptoed out of the room. Of course the minute she was gone we uncovered our eyes and peeked out to see where she was, and watched as she squeezed herself into the hall closet. We kept counting out loud as we carried the steamer trunk which held our toys out of our room and positioned it against the closet door. Then we crumpled up some newspaper, lit an edge of it with a wooden match, and began fanning the smoke under the door with our hands. The smoke was thick and yellow, and I began coughing. "Fire, fire!" we both yelled, trying to sound as frightened as we could while we were laughing.

We turned to run away, to watch what would happen when Jennifer began pounding the door and discovered it wouldn't budge, but instead of the hall wall, we found ourselves pushing against a door while smoke filled up the cramped enclosure where we stood. I don't know how it happened, but instead of Jennifer, *we* were locked inside the smoking closet, and as soon as we figured out where we were, we began screaming in earnest.

It seemed like forever, but it was probably only a matter of seconds before the door opened and we stumbled coughing and crying into the hall. Jennifer stood there, her arms crossed on her chest, looking amused though her eyes flashed. "What you be doin' in there?" she said. "You sposed to be seeking." The steamer trunk was nowhere to be seen.

After lunch, she told us to take a nap, and we swore revenge. She sat in the living room, humming a creepy song, distractedly working on a piece of needlepoint. We decided on the horny toad gambit which had always worked before.

Lance took our pets out of their cage and let them loose in the hall; as usual, they ran frantically for the couch, under which it was dark and cool. "Look out!" we yelled as we ran into the living room. "Horny toads!" Jennifer stopped humming, put down her needlepoint, and watched as the toads slithered over her shoes and under the couch.

"Seems to me two little boys wouldn't be scared of no

horny toads," she said. "Sweet little crawlies is all they are." She got down on her knees and reached under the couch, but what she pulled out was a monstrous enlargement of what we'd let loose. Ten times as big, with a ridge of green armaments down their backs, the lizards looked venomous and carnivorous, and their slippery red tongues darted like flames from their mouths. We shrieked and ran for our room as Jennifer walked toward us holding them out as if offering us to them.

We locked the door and huddled on the upper bunk, and then watched in amazement as she opened the door and entered the room, empty-handed, but no less frightening than if she'd still wielded the lizards. I had to admit, I couldn't remember when I'd had this much fun; adults were more satisfying when they fought back and won. She surveyed the room, and then shook her head as if worried, a reaction which caught my curiosity. "What's the matter?" I said.

"You boys pulling some dangerous shenanigans in here," she said. "I seen little boys on the Islands act this way and they never sing nor dance again. Sometime never even see them again! I don't know, boys. I don't want to scare you little gentlemens, but when horny toads can shake you up . . . "

"That was just a joke," Lance said defensively. "We're not scaredy-cats." Jennifer stared at our closet door, which was closed. "What is it?" Lance said.

She got very quiet and mysterious. "I don't want to put no scare in you boys, 'cause you seem like big mens in little boys' bodies. And there ain't no reason on God's green earth to be scared of nothin' if you always pick the path of good and plenty. So you good little fellows know you ain't got nothin' to be scared of." She paused. "But there be a duppy in your closet."

"Mom won't let us have any fish," I said.

"A duppy not be a fish, don't you know," she said. "A duppy be a spirit!"

Lance and I looked at each other. "Like a ghost?" Lance said.

Jennifer nodded gravely. She sat down on the lower bunk, making the bedspring groan, and patted the bedclothes on either side of her. "Come on down here and sit next to Jennifer," she said. To me, it didn't sound like an invitation. Cautiously we did as we were told.

"Back on the Islands, when somebody die and the body lose his soul, that soul go flying up to Heaven, or go dipping down to the bad place. They be good duppies and they be not-so-good duppies. But the *evil* duppy, he a spirit that got no place to go—can't go up, can't go down. That make the evil duppy mean and he like to frighten little boys. Sometime he hide under beds, and sometime he hide in the closet." I picked up my feet from the floor and hugged my ankles.

"That duppy be a hider and a monster," Jennifer said. "Some of them be so bad a boy can take a look at one in a mirror and turn to a pillar of salt, and all the little animals lick him away to nothing."

"Wow," I said, finally in her power.

But Lance was a year older. "Come on," he said in his best world-weary voice. "There's no such thing as ghosts. I never even heard of a duppy."

"Lots of things little boys ain't never heard of," Jennifer said. "And the bad little boys is the ones the duppies like best. When little boys raise some hooch, the duppies be getting a place ready for them. That's why

some boys do what their elders tell them to.'' I was
ready to swear allegiance, but I could see Lance would
be trouble. "I better be doing some dinner for your
mama.'' She closed the door behind her. I stared at the
closet.

"Don't be such a wuss,'' Lance said. "There's no
such thing as a duppy. She's just trying to scare us into
being good.''

"But what if there is?'' I said, an early indication of
my readiness to accept all possibilities.

"Don't be such a little kid,'' Lance said, the supreme
insult. "There ain't no duppy.''

"Oh, yeah? Show me. Open the closet and show
me.''

"I don't gotta show you nothing,'' Lance said,
haughty as a dowager.

"You chicken?'' I said.

"I ain't chicken.''

"Then open the closet.''

"*You* open the closet,'' he said.

"I already know *I'm* scared,'' I said.

"Come on,'' he said. "We can't let her get us. Let's
play cowboys and Indians.''

So we got our mother's makeup kit and smeared our
faces. Mom had made us throw away Patti's ponytail,
so we used a length of clothesline as a whip; we'd need it
later to tie up Jennifer. We got our dart guns and darts,
put on our camouflage pants, and snuck down the hall
to look for our prey. Jennifer had her back to us; the
heavy smell of frying bananas hung in the air. She
shook her shoulders as she stood there, humming her
creepy song.

"Go,'' Lance said, and we went. I rattled the sound

of a machine gun from my throat, and Lance made a series of piercing war whoops as we ran pell-mell into the kitchen, firing darts at random.

What we found wasn't Jennifer; what we found changed the course of our young lives. Instead of a toothy, smiling Jamaican woman we found three Sioux warriors in full headdress and warpaint. They were lean and dark-skinned, streaked with ocher and vermilion, and from the quivers on their backs they pulled arrows tipped with real arrowheads and began firing them at us; they whistled past us and stuck with a *thunk* into the plasterboard behind us. We whipped around in terror, dropping our dart guns, and ran toward the dining room.

But the rest of the war party had beaten us to it, and we met another barrage of arrows from that direction. The air was filled with wild whoops of vengeance; and under that, from somewhere, came the monotonous beat of a drum. Four more braves stood up from their concealed position behind the couch, and the tips of their arrows were flaming; one streaked by me and set the living room drapes on fire.

Lance grabbed me and pulled me out of my terrified trance; together we dodged and hustled and were almost to our room when the door at the end of the hall burst open, the door to our mother's room, and a chief astride a pinto pony came crashing at us, a spear in his upraised arm. We yelled and bashed into our room. Arrows thudded against the door we slammed and locked behind us and, looking for a place to hide, we headed for the closet.

Lance, my boyhood idol, had been wrong, and I

resolved not to follow his chaotic lead any longer. We opened the closet wide only to slam it shut again, screaming. My intuition, as I should have known, had been right all along. There *was* such a thing as a duppy.

My mother got home much later than usual that night, and though Jennifer had been due to leave at five-thirty, she stayed with us, even fed us some supper. When my mother opened the door, she stood listening to the quiet as though she thought we all three must be dead. Jennifer sat in the big easy chair, doing her needlepoint, and humming her Island tune which no longer seemed creepy but instead a secret song of the initiates my brother and I had become. We were sprawled on the floor at her feet, drawing pictures of Indians and duppies, humming along with her.

"Hi, Mom," Lance said. "How was work?"

"Who's being punished?" my mother asked.

"Nobody, missy," Jennifer said, getting to her feet.

"They weren't any trouble?" my mother asked.

"Oh my, no," Jennifer said. "These is two *good* little gentlemens."

My mother was speechless. Jennifer beamed as she packed up her needlepoint, discreetly stuffing the bills my mother gave her into the bag along with the colored threads.

"Will you come back tomorrow, Jennifer?" I asked.

"Please?" Lance said, possibly the first time he'd uttered that syllable without coercion.

"But that's up to the missy," Jennifer said. "You gentlemens know that."

"Could Jennifer come back tomorrow?" I asked.

"Please, Mom?" Lance said.

"Well, of *course*," my mother said, totally mystified.

"And can we play some more games?" Lance asked Jennifer.

"Yeah," I said. "Some more of the imaginaries?" I shivered, remembering how it had felt to be tied to the stakes in the living room carpet, the flames rising around us, the Indians yelling and whooping in a circle.

Jennifer bent over and put a hand on each of us. "Now you don't need old Jennifer to play them imaginaries. All those tings be right in the noodles." She tapped my head with her forefinger. "You just remember you don't need to fuss and trouble and give old people the pain in the head. Now you give old Jennifer a kiss goodbye."

We kissed her smooth, warm cheeks and then, holding her hands, we saw her to the door. My mother, dazed, walked into the kitchen and Lance followed her, saying, "Guess what, Mom?"

But I stayed behind to watch Jennifer leave. What I saw didn't surprise me, even if Lance, later that night, said he didn't believe a word I said. My father and mother were divorced, for good, and we'd never have life again the way it once had been. And my mother worked now, full-time, so we'd have to learn to be more independent. But we had a good head start, I thought. We knew about the imaginaries.

I watched as Jennifer walked down the drive toward the street, where no car waited. But before she reached the circle of the nearest streetlight she faded from view, the way frost disappears under the morning sun. The night sky was scattered with stars and I heard the faint whisper of that lovely wordless song, as if from the heavens.

SANTA '85
by Steven Bauer

Based on the Universal Television series *Amazing Stories*
Created by Steven Spielberg
Adapted from the episode ''Santa '85''
Teleplay by Joshua Brand and John Falsey
Story by Steven Spielberg

WHEN, EXACTLY, WE AS A PEOPLE FIRST BECAME CYN-
ical is a matter of some dispute, but no one would argue
the fact that simple loss of faith is a serious social problem. Elected officials know this, for we have, by and
large, lost faith in government; we have lost faith, many
of us, in the captains of business and industry, in our
educational institutions, and in the police. And loss of
faith in organized religion has troubled theologians for
longer than most would wish to acknowledge.

But perhaps no institution has so badly suffered in
this regard as the one-man good will and peace initiative
known as Santa Claus. Why so few young people still
believe in him is a question, fortunately, which doesn't
bother the old man himself; in fact, for the most part
he's not even aware there *is* a problem.

Last Christmas Eve, for example, though his wife
tried to warn him that not everyone in the world shared
his simple faith in the goodness of human nature . . .

The wind-driven snow piled against his door, and the
old man was almost ready to be off. As always, there

were last-minute details to check, for he held himself
responsible for nothing less than the world's happiness,
a rather large responsibility. His wife had let out the
waist of his pants, and now, with him in them, was ad-
justing them so they were neither too loose nor too
snug, while he went over his itinerary. But his enthu-
siasm for his job soon had him smiling hugely and rubbing his chubby red hands together.

"Oh, what a great night its going to be," Mr. Claus
said.

"Not if you don't hold still," his wife said, jabbing
him with a pin. He yelled and withdrew as far as he
could inside his bright red trousers, but she held him
tight. "Some sight it would be if your pants fell down in
the midst of a delivery," she said.

"This suit wasn't supposed to shrink, you now," he
said.

"It didn't, dear. If you don't stay away from the
cookies, I'll have to put a stretchband on these trousers."

But her husband wasn't listening; he was mentally
checking items off on a list. "Steve Heptinstall, Roa-
noke, Virginia," he said. "Did I pack his catcher's
mitt?"

"Yes, dear," his wife said.

"Claire Rinfret, Paris, France. Did I . . . ?"

"Yes, dear."

"My mittens," Mr. Claus said.

"They're on the mantel where you put them," his
wife said.

"By the way," he said, "while you were out feeding
the reindeer, one of those elves called, inviting us to
spend New Year's Day with them."

"In Hollywood?" Mrs. Claus said. "No thanks. Far too much neon. And if you ask me, they're just a bunch of sellouts."

"One must earn a living, my dear." He bustled into his coat, took a look in the full-length mirror, and couldn't restrain himself. "Oh, I'm so excited," he said. "I can't wait to get out there and see all those smiling, happy faces."

"Just remember, dear," Mrs. Claus said. "The world has changed over the last several hundred years. You read the newspapers; you see what's on the evening news. It's a modern, sophisticated world out there."

"Are you saying I haven't kept up with it?"

"No," his wife said. "You have, in your own way. It's just that people don't believe in things the way they used to. Like Christmas. Or Santa." She almost whispered the last two words.

"Horsefeathers!" the old man said. "Even in the worst of times children remembered me, waited up for me, and did I let them down?"

"No, dear," his wife said. "You didn't."

"Maybe some didn't get what they asked for," Mr. Claus admitted. "But I did the job. I delivered. And with a personal touch, mind you. So my philosophy is . . ."

"*The more things change, the more they stay the same,*" his wife said.

Mr. Claus winked and began to laugh and just then, while his wife still stood there with her needle and thread, one of his buttons popped off.

Mrs. Claus kissed him goodbye, but he was so preoccupied with his upcoming journey, he almost didn't kiss

her back. "Watch out for the 747s," she said. "And
don't go sneaking up on any air traffic controllers like
you did last year. Have you got your list?" He slapped
his back pocket and nodded. "Have you checked it
twice?"

"Don't *worry*," Mr. Claus said. "Everything's in
order." He opened the front door and snow slapped his
face. "This is going to be the greatest Christmas since
1492," he said. He moved through the picket fence's
gate and gave a loud whistle. From a barn eight tiny
reindeer came galloping, pulling a large sleigh. His wife,
shivering in the doorway, waved. "Have a grand time,"
she called.

"I'll be home by noon tomorrow," Mr. Claus said.
"Now Dasher! Now Dancer! Now Donner! And
Vixen!" The sleigh lurched forward into the driving
blizzard, the bells attached to the reindeers' leads jingling brightly. "Ho ho ho," Mr. Claus called, to no
one. "*Merry Christmas*!"

The town of Larchmont is in a territorial division of
local government known as Westchester County, which
in turn is contained by the state of New York in the
United States of America, but what gives Larchmont
and surrounding communities such as Mamaroneck and
Scarsdale their character is their proximity to that
metropolis known as New York City, to which a great
number of Westchester County's wage-earners travel
each day in order to carry out their occupations as doc-
tors, stockbrokers, lawyers, and businessmen. By and
large the families here are prosperous and live in richly
appointed houses, filled with both the most modern and
sophisticated of furnishings and appliances as well as

the treasures of the past, known locally as antiques. Having so many material goods makes these people, by and large, suspicious of strangers, even ones who say "Ho ho ho."

And being at a latitude approximately 41 degrees north of the equator and 73 degrees, 50 minutes west of Greenwich, Westchester County, during the months of December through March, has a fair chance of snow. On December 24, 1985, it lay under four inches of new powder, just enough to make driving a little tricky and to make dreams of a white Christmas come true.

In his bedroom, Bobby Mynes, eight years old, was suffering from the same lack of belief afflicting so many of his countrymen. His mother and father attended him, his mother pulling up the cuff of white sheet to his chin, his father standing with arms crossed.

"*Of course* there's a Santa Claus," his mother said.

"That's not what Jed and Jeff said," Bobby objected.

"Jed and Jeff Marshall are just teasing you because they're older."

"Really?" Bobby asked.

"That's right," his father said.

"But Nancy Benedict said it too, and she's the same age as me." Mr. and Mrs. Mynes stole a glance at one another; Mr. Mynes shrugged.

"Well," said his mother. "I guess the Marshall boys must have talked to her too."

"Yeah," Bobby said, turning on his side. He didn't seem convinced.

"I'd keep your eyes peeled tonight, Bobby," his father said. "You never know who you might see on Christmas Eve."

His parents said good night, wished him a merry Christmas, and closed the door behind them. As soon as they were gone, Bobby leaned over and rescued a toy dart gun he'd hidden under the bed, loaded it, and fired at a poster of Clint Eastwood as Dirty Harry which hung on the sloping bedroom ceiling. The dart hit Cliff's square chin and stuck. It's frustrating being a doubting eight-year-old.

He was sleeping when the sleigh landed gently on the roof, when the loud clip-clop of boots moved across the shingles to the chimney. Mr. Claus peered down into the sooty darkness, but as he lowered his face, his nose brushed the thick metal grid the Mynes had installed to restrain runaway sparks and cinders. He tried to pull it loose, but it had been mortared in place, and besides, although Mr. Claus didn't know it, it saved him the humiliation of having gotten stuck in this particular chimney.

He tossed a huge sack of toys into the soft snow and then slid down a drainpipe, right past Bobby's window. But the boy didn't awaken. Who knows what went on behind those closed eyelids? Visions of sugarplums? Gobots and Transformers, more likely.

Mr. Claus was now faced with a situation becoming more and more familiar to him. Like a common burglar, he searched for an unbolted window and, glad to find one, he raised it, swung his bag of toys inside, and then heaved his ungainly bulk over the sill. He stood and listened, but not a living creature was stirring, not even the gerbil burrowed under wood chips in his cage in the kitchen.

An electronic creature, however, *was* stirring, blinking its single eye. Westchester County, as mentioned before, is ripe for the picking; thus many of its inhabitants have invested in state-of-the-art security devices, another capitalist venture born in the wave of disbelief whose first cousin is paranoia.

Mr. and Mrs. Mynes were in their bedroom wrapping presents when Mr. Claus tripped the electric eye; the burglar alarm panel blinked on, and its high squeal sounded. Seconds later, the Mynes's phone rang. "Safetech Security," a robotic voice said. "May I have your abort code?"

"Five-seven-two-three," Mr. Mynes said. "Call the police." He hung up, reached for the alarm panel, and punched a red button.

Mr. Claus, a trusting soul, never knew what hit him. As he was on his hands and knees putting presents under the tree, floodlights blared on, and from the stereo speakers a shrill automated voice shrieked, "Help! Call the police! Help! Help! Illegal entry! Police! Help!"

Mr. Claus stood up, bewildered. Blinded and disoriented by the lights, he grabbed his bag and stumbled toward what he thought was the front door; but he blundered instead into Bobby Mynes's bedroom. The boy sat bolt upright in bed, aimed the dart gun, and fired, hitting Mr. Claus square in the forehead.

Staring at the child, the traitor, the man backed up, right into the waiting arms of Mr. Mynes. "Get away from my son," the man yelled, fueled by television stories of child abuse and kidnaping. Mr. Mynes tried to grapple the man to the ground, but he couldn't fasten his arms around Mr. Claus's belly.

"Be patient," Mr. Claus remonstrated. "There's plenty for everyone." He broke free, like the Refrigerator, and rumbled toward the front of the house where he flung open the door into a sudden explosion of blinding spotlights. An authoritative male voice, a perfect imitation of a television policeman, said "Freeze!" It *was* cold, but Mr. Claus, after all, came from the North Pole, and had no intention of doing any such thing.

It was Sheriff Horace Smivey, of the Larchmont Police, and he *was* imitating a TV policeman, Patrolman Andrew Renko. "Drop your bag and raise those mittens!" he said.

Bobby Mynes, in his bathrobe and slippers and accompanied by his distraught parents, raced out into the lights and the new snow. Mr. Claus turned toward the boy who'd so recently assaulted him and forgave him; he'd been frightened, the little tyke. Who wouldn't have been with that insane voice yelling "Help!" from the living room? He smiled, his cheeks red as polished apples, his long beard white as the driven snow, and his eyes twinkled as he winked at Bobby. Given another few seconds, his belly might have shook like a bowl full of jelly. And at that moment, as at the moment in Disney's *Peter Pan* when Peter asks for help in reviving Tinker Bell, Bobby Mynes *believed*.

They cuffed Mr. Claus and hustled him toward a large van.

"Mom," Bobby said. "It's *him*. You better let him go."

"It's cold out here," Mrs. Mynes said. "Let's get inside."

The police flung open the doors of the van, and three skinny men, reeking of cheap whiskey, all dressed in outlandish red costumes trimmed with fake white fur, with fake cotton beards and jaunty red caps, opened their arms to Mr. Claus. "Come on in," one yelled. "The more the merrier. What a great costume."

As they drove away toward the jail, Bobby Mynes tried to explain to his parents, who, like reasonable adults all over the world, didn't much listen to children.

Wetherby, twenty-three and new to the Larchmont force, drove, while Smivey, bless his cynical bejowled soul, rode shotgun and grumbled, as usual, about being overworked and underpaid. The three men dressed to look like Mr. Claus had fallen asleep; only Mr. Claus himself remained concerned about his new mode of transit. He gripped the wire screen separating him from Wetherby and Smivey, trying to stand upright as the van bounced over the snowy road.

"How many houses you hit tonight, fella?" Smivey asked.

"About forty million so far," Mr. Claus said. "Give or take a million." Smivey rolled his eyes and smirked at Wetherby. "So you can imagine," Mr. Claus continued, "I've still a big night ahead. Hardly scratched the earth's surface. Have we much further to go?"

"In a hurry to be locked up?" Smivey asked.

"Actually," Mr. Claus said, "I'm on a practically impossible schedule, and I'd appreciate getting back to my sleigh as quickly as possible. The population is growing so. Mrs. Claus can let out this coat an inch or two every year, but she can't put a stretchband on the trousers of the world. Ho ho ho!"

Smivey whipped around, offended. "No laughing,"

he growled, as though it were a new ordinance in Larchmont. "Nothing funny ever happens in this car unless I say so, right, Wetherby?"

"Yes, sir," Wetherby said, though his tone was less than enthusiastic.

"Yes, sir, *Sheriff Smivey*," Smivey said, and Wetherby complied.

"Smivey?" Mr. Claus said. "You wouldn't happen to be Leonard Smivey's boy Horace, would you?"

"How'd you know that, pops?"

"Actually," Mr. Claus said, consulting his list. "Your house was going to be next."

Trying to raise the spirits in the van (and trying to annoy Smivey, if the truth were told), Wetherby began singing "Jingle Bells," and Claus joined in.

"Knock it off and make a left," Smivey growled. "I hate that song, and I hate these decorations."

"You know," Mr. Claus said, "it seems to me you have no Christmas spirit."

"Why should I?" Smivey said. "It's just another day, one out of three-sixty-five. My spirit's right up there with armed robbery, vagrancy, and drunk driving, all symptoms of holiday cheer."

"Sounds fairly awful," Mr. Claus said.

"You don't know the half of it," Smivey said.

Bobby Mynes shot darts at Clint Eastwood. "Bobby Mynes, you listen to me," his mother said.

"You're wrong," Bobby said.

"Every Christmas," his mother said, "a few very sad old men try to . . ."

"It was Santa," Bobby said.

". . . rob those people who are richer than they."

"He wasn't robbing, Mom. He was *giving*. And you and Dad arrested him like he was some terrorist or something."

His mother cocked her head, as though she heard something in the distance. "Listen," she said.

"You guys are in big trouble," Bobby said. "Free him *now*." He would have felt right at home during the sixties.

"Aren't those sleighbells I hear?" Mrs. Mynes said. Bobby groaned. "Quick, get into bed. Santa's coming."

"But he's already *been* here."

"Now be very quiet," his mother said, "and if you're lucky you might see him." His mother tiptoed out, a cartoon of quiet. As the bedroom light went out, the curtains behind Bobby's head were filled with the silhouettes of eight tiny reindeer.

Down at the station, Mr. Claus was having his mug shot taken, straight on, right profile, left profile. Wetherby finished fingerprinting the three drunk Santas. "For crying out loud," Sheriff Smivey said. "What's taking so long? I haven't got all night."

"Are you really serious about booking these poor guys on Christmas Eve, sir?" Wetherby asked.

"You bet I am."

"But they're just a couple of harmless guys who were lonely and got a little drunk."

"Book them," Smivey snarled. "Next!"

Next was Mr. Claus. He rose with as much dignity as he could muster and approached Patrolman Wetherby, who said, "Forefinger, right hand, please."

Mr. Claus presented his hand to Wetherby to do with

as he wished. "I'd like a word with you, Horace," he said, "about your Christmas spirit."

"Save it for the judge," Smivey said.

"Right thumb, please."

"Will you be spending Christmas Eve with your family, Horace?" Mr. Claus asked.

"Sheriff's not married," Wetherby said, taking Mr. Claus's left hand.

"What about with some friends?" Mr. Claus asked.

"Hasn't got any," Wetherby mumbled.

"Didn't your family ever celebrate Christmas?" Mr. Claus asked.

"Sheriff never had a family," Wetherby said. "He grew up in an orphanage."

"Writing my biography?" Smivey said.

"No, sir."

"You got anything else you want to say?"

"No, sir."

"Good," Smivey said. "Keep it that way. Let's go," he said, grabbing Mr. Claus and leading him from the room. Wetherby picked up the sheet on which he'd pressed the man's ink-smeared fingers. The little squares designating each print were blank. He raised the card to the light, but no marks appeared. "What's going on here?" he said.

Dressed in his G. I. Joe commando outfit, and carrying his dart gun, Bobby Mynes crawled out his bedroom window into a snowdrift. Some snow got into his boots, but he wasn't about to be deterred by a little discomfort; he had a job to do. "Come on, you guys," he said. "That's right, this way."

The reindeer obeyed him. Their harness bells began to

jingle as they picked up speed, and Bobby could hear
the delicate patter of their tiny hooves as he climbed into
the sleigh and the nine of them were off, toward the
town jail.

"Who are these poor fellows, Sheriff Smivey?" Mr.
Claus asked with real concern, pointing to the men
dressed in clothes meant to resemble his own, who now
lay in various states of disarray on three mattresses.

"That one's a drunk and disorderly from the Way-
farer's Tavern," Smivey said, pointing. "And that one
passed out in the hospital before he could give the presents to the children in the ward. And that miserable
creep was caught stealing decorations from the department store where he's worked for the past week."

Mr. Claus shook his head, genuinely troubled. "Usually the first time a child believes in something other
than his own mother and father is when he tells his true
heart's desire to one of these bearded over-stuffed
strangers. Funny thing is, these men who dress up as
Santa usually have no children of their own. And the
sadness of Christmas being almost over for another year
has delivered each of them to this unfortunate place.
People *believed* in them, Horace."

"You got that right, old-timer," Smivey said.

"Did I ever let you down, Sheriff?"

Smivey looked at Mr. Claus, and thought about a
time when he *had* believed; it made him feel even worse.
"You were just the first of many disappointments."

In as kindly a voice as he had, Mr. Claus said, "Do
you care to tell me about it?"

"I was just a kid," Smivey said, "when I wrote Santa
a letter—nine pages single-spaced—telling him I'd been

good as could be. Brushed every tooth, did all my chores, and all I asked him for was one Buck Rogers green toy ray gun." He swung open the cell door toward which he'd been leading the old man.

"And you didn't get it?" Santa said. He smiled at Horace Smivey, and something old and rusty tried to jolt to life in Smivey's breast. "Sometimes even Santa makes mistakes," the old man said.

Smivey's heart was racing now, and his hands fumbled with the lock. But his good sense got the better of him, and his eyes narrowed and his heart slowed. "Nah," he said. "Nah, this is crazy. It can't be. Y'hear me? You can't be. Get in there."

He clanged the metal door shut and stalked down the hall toward the main office and Wetherby. Mournfully, Mr. Claus watched him go. "Just what this sorry old world needs," he said. "Christmas without Santa."

If you've been following this story closely, you'll remember there's a character we haven't heard from in a while. His small hands suddenly appeared gripping the bars of the window separating Santa Claus from the outside world. Mr. Claus didn't see him at first, having fallen into a state of despondency from which he couldn't shake himself since two of the fake Santas were leaning against him, snoring. "Santa, it's me, Bobby Mynes," the boy whispered. "I'm going to get you out." He tied one end of a very thick rope to the jailhouse window and the other end to the back of the sleigh. Clint Eastwood had taught him this.

Meanwhile Horace Smivey and Wetherby were engaged in an altercation concerning the missing fingerprints. "You sure you printed the guy?" Smivey said.

"Positive, sir," Wetherby said.

"I've just about had enough from this old geezer," Smivey said. "Come on." They arrived at the door of the cell just as Bobby raised two fingers to his mouth and whistled. On cue, the reindeer bucked and charged forward, the rope grew more and more taut, and under the tension and force of the reindeer, the window began to pull loose. It happened slowly at first, as a dam bursting loose begins with a single crack, but then the whole wall burst open, bricks flying in all directions. All four Santas ran through the gap in the wall, the three bogus ones scattering, Mr. Claus himself running to the sleigh. Smivey stood there in fury and amazement as the sleigh, with Bobby Mynes and the old geezer in the driver's seat, began to gain momentum, pulling a barred window down Main Street.

The sleigh rattled and clanged passed parked cars and closed and shuttered shops until Bobby was able to untie the rope; luckily there was no traffic out, due to the snow, the date, and the fact that it was 2 A.M. It was grand driving along like that until they heard the cruiser. After them, siren blaring, red lights flashing, skidding and snarling, came Horace Smivey.

The reindeer picked up speed, but so did Smivey. "Quick," Bobby yelled. "He's gaining on us." Santa cracked his whip and steered the sleigh into a snow-covered town park. Undeterred in his desire to put this guy, this fake, this supreme con who'd almost made him believe, in the slammer for a while, Smivey spun his wheel, fishtailed round two corners, and swerved the cruiser into the park's opposite entrance. The sleigh was crossing a meadow and Smivey left the macadam and accelerated directly for the old man and the boy.

"Hold on, Bobby," Santa yelled. For just as it seemed the patrol car would cut them off, the first brace of reindeer took to the air, as though their hooves climbed a gentle invisible incline, and the others followed gracefully in line; the sleigh, loaded with presents for all the world, swooped over Horace Smivey's head, leaving on his upturned face an expression of wonder and the drifting spray of snow from the sleigh's runners. He'd been unable to admit it back at the jail, but for a moment there he'd gotten the feeling it *had* been Santa, and when there'd been no fingerprints on the sheet . . .

Here was proof irrefutable. He stared up into the black sky swept with stars as the sleigh grew smaller and smaller; he heard the faint "Ho ho ho" of the man he'd arrested, and then he saw something plummeting to earth.

It hit the ground at his feet; he picked it up as carefully, as gently as though it were a bomb. But it was a present, wrapped in paper of a kind he hadn't seen since he was a kid. And inside was a green Buck Rogers ray gun, the kind they'd sold in 1933, an antique.

Smivey's throat caught and tears streamed down his cheeks, so when he looked again at the sky, he saw smeared stars and four sleighs disappearing south toward Manhattan. And that old rusty engine called *belief* started pushing his heart's pistons once again.

The story of faith returning to a young boy and a middle-aged bachelor may not solve the problems of our time, but it's a beginning. The politicians and the educators, the law enforcement officers and churchmen will simply have to work to emulate the cheer and selflessness of Mr. Claus, which would be refreshing, don't you think?

How Bobby Mynes got home that night, and what his parents said to him—they didn't believe he'd rescued Santa Claus, but they were adults after all, cynical, paranoid, the owners of a Safetech Security System—well, that's another story.

ONE FOR THE ROAD
by Steven Bauer

Based on the Universal Television series *Amazing Stories*
Created by Steven Spielberg
Adapted from the episode ''One for the Road''
Written by James D. Bissell

I CAN TELL A TALL TALE WITH THE BEST OF THEM, BUT on everything holy I swear this happened, the honest truth, first word to last, so help me God. It was 1934, the South Bronx, and the winter was fierce in New York. Times was bad, the Great Depression. I was lucky to have a job, even as a bartender at Maroni's. Lots of guys weren't anywhere near as lucky.

Tony, the owner, wasn't a bad sort, just worried about making it through. His place had been a speak-easy just a couple months before, and though selling booze was legal now, Maroni's was still sleazy. Most of the time, I polished glasses and swept the floor and told the regulars no more credit and yelled at the red-suited gent from the Salvation Army.

He came in every afternoon—who could blame him? —to get out of the cold. Snow swept across the little corner he'd chosen, right by the door to the bar, and we heard the monotonous clang of his bell like a death's knell, on and on.

Who could blame anyone? All of us was hard up— Daniel McLaren who worked as a salesman at a time when no one was buying, Francis Pearse, an undertaker with plenty of corpses and no one to pay for their proper disposal. Me, I worked partly for tips, and they wasn't what you'd call plentiful. And Tony was so worried he started chalking the bottles and comparing them to the day's receipts. He took to watching every drink I poured, and me a soft touch with a heart of gold. It was hard on a man.

It was a Friday afternoon in late December, the worst time of the year, when the whole thing started. Work was over for the week, with nothing but two long days ahead to think about how Christmas was right around the corner and us with no money in our pockets. Francis sat at the bar, his hands folded; Dan hadn't got there yet; Mike Malloy, an old sot in his late sixties, was snoring face down in a puddle of beer. He picked up his head, grinned as only a total souse can grin, and collapsed with a thud.

The noise made Maroni look up. "Ask the gentleman if he wants a drink," he said; I snorted, and didn't laugh.

That's when the door opened and the Salvation Army guy came in. Before he could say a word, I said, "We gave at the office."

"Won't you help those who are worse off than yourself?" he said.

"Sure," Tony said. "Sit down and get warm. Then come check this inventory. All the free drinks these lollipops con me out of, ain't nobody worse off than me." In a little while we heard the mournful bell tolling outside again.

Tony turned back to his work, studying the rye, and Francis looked at me beseechingly. Like I said, I'm a soft touch. But I have my fun too. Quiet as I can, I pour

a shot of whiskey and let it sit on the bar, all lonely.
When Francis reaches for it, I slide it away and say,
"Two bits." He jerks back his hand and looks at me
like I'm a dog that just bit him. "Of course," he says,
patting his suit, pocket by pocket.

McLaren arrives right then, takes off his coat, and
heads for the drink. "Thanks, Joe," he says. But I get it
away from him too. It's like the shell game, only better;
my hand is faster than their hands. "Two bits," I say.

Meanwhile Francis is patting up and down like he's a
cop frisking himself. Then he shrugs and says—get this-
—"Ah, good bartender. *Let him drink, and forget his
poverty, and remember his misery no more.*" This
makes even Malloy open his eyes. "Proverbs 31 verse
7," Francis says, a real good Catholic.

Dan is looking miserable too, more than usual. He
fumbles in his pocket for a cigarette, and I see his hands
shaking. "How do you think it feels to go home to three
kids and a wife with no money in the wallet? *You*"—
here he points to me—"don't know a thing about it."
He's right; I ain't married.

"To see those bright young eyes beginning to wither
with despair," he says. "Christmas just around the corner, and I can offer them nothing; not even a quarter
for the moving picture show. All I can do is put on a
smile and buck up their hope." He's beginning to get to
me; my cheeks are tightening up like when I get emo-
tional. "Please give me that drink, Joe. It helps me to
lie. That's all I got right now."

I can feel Tony looking at me, but I push the drink at
McLaren anyway. "Take it out of my salary," I say,
over my shoulder. Even Malloy is impressed with this,
enough to come out of his stupor and knock over a

barstool. It falls to the floor with a crash. So does he.

But see what you get when you're nice? Right away Francis starts in. "I bury every cheap hood and petty thief in the Bronx and when I go to collect, it's a destitute widow offering me her pathetic body or some diseased street thug wants to hoist me up. I'm owed a great deal, out of the charity of my own heart, let me tell you."

From the floor Mike Malloy heaved into view. He had a way with verses he'd memorized; even when almost unconscious he could make them sound pretty:

> "To fret o'er life's terrible fate,
>   Or bemoan o'er that which is,
> Will only bring despair and hate
>   For *death's* where justice lives."

He belched, lurched forward, put both hands on the bar. With a boozy grin he said, "Which way, deary, to the loo?"

"You don't know by now," Maroni says, "you deserve to piss your pants." Malloy staggered off.

"Better times, you know I'd stand you to a drink, Francis," Maroni says. "You been a good customer." He sighed real deep, maybe meaning it. "You know, a little money wouldn't hurt any of us. But I don't know nobody these days that's got it easy." From the W.C. the voice of Malloy rose in somber, boozy song.

"Did a funeral the other day," Francis says. "This guy named Al Compinari. His old lady left him to shack up with Toots O'Connor. Then she finds out there's a contract on her husband. They're still legally hitched, see. So what does she do? She takes out a hefty in-

surance policy and four days later becomes a rich griev-
ing widow when Compinari is accidentally run over by
a truck.'' From the W.C. comes the sound of a door
banging and Malloy hacking up his tubercular lungs.

It was a good story; we all were listening. Dan says,
''Seems like a fair way to earn a few bucks. Guy was
gonna die anyway.''

''She might have told him!'' Francis exploded. ''He
might not of croaked.''

Maroni, the realist, says, ''Look how much better off
she is now.''

''She didn't even give him a decent box. Plain pine,
no upholstery, the cheapest. I know,'' Francis says,
thumping his chest.

''I don't see nothing wrong in taking advantage of a
little inside information,'' I says. ''No reason to spend
the profits needlessly.'' Francis looks at me like I'm a
snake; Dan nods approval, but he's the one I gave the
free drink to.

So Malloy comes back, weaving, coughing, and
singing a song I ain't heard before:

> ''I've seen the funeral of my hopes,
>   Entombed them one by one;
>   No tear was shed, no word was said—
>   The solemn task was done.''

''Pipe down, Malloy,'' says Tony. As if on cue,
Malloy burps and falls to the floor. Tony shakes his
head, real sorrowful. ''Most of the bums that hang
around here are going to die. Malloy's been trying to
drink himself to death for two years now. He'll probably succeed too, especially in this weather.''

Always the professional, Francis looks at Malloy like he's ready for embalming. "But don't count on him to have money to pay for his funeral," Francis says. "He'll be like all the others."

"That's true," Maroni says. "His wife's dead, he's got no friends. You'll find no one who cares enough about him to pay for one."

Francis says, " 'A useless life is an early death.' Goethe." The showoff.

"About the only way to pay for the poor sot's funeral," Tony says, drumming his fingers on the bar and staring at Malloy, "would be a life insurance policy."

First we look at each other.

Then we look at Malloy on the floor. For a minute it seems he's stopped breathing, but then we can see some of his whiskers moving and his belly going up and down a little. All of us was filled with gladness, let me tell you; we thought of Malloy all of a sudden with new affection.

I was polishing glasses that night when Dan came in, smug as if he just got lucky. Malloy was passed out on the bar and Francis was staring at the wallpaper, off somewhere in boozeland.

Like he owns the place, Dan pours himself a drink, but Tony, who walks in from the back, doesn't say a word, because everything's changed now. Malloy lurches to life at the sound of liquor being poured and says with a slur, "Kin' sir. Would you share a bit of liquid magic with a poor old man not long for this worl'?" or some such tripe.

"Why certainly, Mr. Malloy," Dan says, liberally sloshing some rotgut gin in a glass. Then he pulls something from his jacket pocket; the rustle of legal-sized parchment jolts old Francis out of his trance.

"How in the world?" I say.

"Hard times, brother," Dan says. "You can get a lot for a little." He turns to Malloy who stares at the swirl of gin and ice like it holds a burning fire. "Mr. Malloy?" Dan says, as humble and respectful as you please. "I have here a petition to the Mayor protesting the abominable conditions suffered by poor orphan children in the New York sweatshops. I'd be most obliged if you'd sign it and help us let our voice be heard."

Malloy looks at him carefully, as if trying to sight down the barrel of a gun. "Oh, the poor tykes. Misser McLaren, I'd be prou . . . uurpp! . . . proud to, if you'll jus' show me where. I can't see too well, you unnerstan'."

"Just sign here," Dan says, giving Malloy a fountain pen and pointing to the dotted line marked Insured. The old man scrawls his name and Dan whips the form out from under him and waves it in the air, drying the ink. "*Thank* you, Mr. Malloy; the orphans thank you."

"You're very welcome, my good man," Malloy says. "May I perpose a celebertory toas'?"

"Of course," Dan says. This time he fills the glass three-quarters full. "To the orphans," he says.

Malloy picks up the glass with two hands and thirstily drinks it down; then he falls backwards, like a toppled tree.

The instant he hits the floor, Tony says, "You got it? And you got him to sign it?" With a flourish Dan shows us the policy; there's poor Malloy's John Hancock, like he signed his own death warrant.

"You got it!" yells Francis.

"Shhh," Tony says. "You'll wake up Malloy."

"I don't think we have to worry about that," I says. The guy, after all, just drank a fifth of gin, just about.

"We got him signed, sealed, delivered," Dan says. "Considering the, uh, commission, our broker most prudently waived the medical examination. Upon the timely demise of Mr. Michael Clancy Malloy, we'll all be wealthy men."

"How long do you think it'll take?" Francis asks.

"I'm not a doctor," Maroni says. "But it can't be too much longer. The *idea* of his liver is enough to make you die."

"He's been trying to drink himself to death ever since I started," I say, "and considering our resources"—here I point to all Maroni's bottles shining in the light from the mirror—"we should be able to help our friend along."

Then Dan, sport that he is, suggests a toast to Malloy, and we all drink his health, in a funny sort of way.

By the third week in January Tony was desperate. We'd told Malloy he had a tab, and he was running it. There were cases of empty bottles, of gin, of vodka, of whiskey and wine. Though we told Tony we'd all reimburse him for his help with the booze, he was the one out of pocket, after all.

We'd spent a lot of time drinking *with* Malloy, and we all felt the worse for it. Dan had veins popping all over his cheeks and nose; Francis had given three funerals while totally stoned. Now Dan was passed out on the bar and Malloy was coming back for more, polite as the day he was born. "Misser Maroni, sir," he said.

"Might a poor man such as myself have another drink?"

I could see Tony was about to throttle the guy so I says, "Certainly, Mr. Malloy." Now I've seen soaks, and I've seen stews, but I ain't never seen anyone close to Malloy. That man could drink a case of booze and still crawl out the door. I emptied yet one more bottle into his bottomless glass.

"Blesh you, Joe," he says to me. "Iss friffully col' outside and a man needs a lill forshificashun jus' thinking of it." He raised his glass to me and said, "You'll put this on my tab?" He swallowed it down, smiled blissfully, and fell backwards off his stool.

"He's going to drink me dry," Tony Maroni said. "I don't believe it."

So Francis comes in, black as a crow from a funeral. When he sees Malloy stretched out, his face brightens and he rushes over and puts his ear to the sot's chest. Then he stands up and says, "He's not dead," the saddest words he's ever uttered.

"No," Tony says, "but *we're* almost completely broke. In the past three weeks he's drunk twenty-seven bottles of rye, fourteen bottles of vodka, and five bottles of Scotch. Every time he passes out I'm sure he's done for, but he just gets up, apologizes, and says he's thirsty."

"He's got to die soon," Francis says. "I need the money."

"*You* need the money? We may all be out in the snow with Mr. Malloy before too long," Tony says.

"Maybe we should just give him beer," Francis says. "My father used to tell me, God rest his soul, if you give an Irishman lager for a month, he's a dead man. An Irishman's lined with copper and the beer corrodes it. Whiskey polishes the copper and is the saving of him."

"You should know," I say. "But we can't wait another month."

"What if we did corrode his pipes a little?" Tony asks, real quiet. "Maybe we've been too kind to Mr. Malloy. Perhaps something a little stronger would speed him on his way."

"Like what?" I say.

"Some wood alcohol," Tony says.

"But that will kill him," Francis says, all self-righteous.

"Francis," I say. Meanwhile Tony goes into the back room.

"But . . . isn't this . . . murder?" Francis says, real innocent.

"Of course not, Francis," I say, pouring him a drink on the house. "Look at him. You think it'll make any difference to him if it's rubbing alcohol or Jameson's?" The good undertaker began to look resigned to our evil ways. "Besides," I say, "it'll speed things up. You know," I say. "The money."

Francis looks at Malloy and says, " 'It is not death, but dying, which is terrible.' Fielding, 1751." I'm about to bust the pompous ass when Tony comes back, his eyebrows bunched up.

"All I can find is kerosene," he says. Francis turns white as a poisonous mushroom, and even I am taken aback. "Let's pour it into this bottle," Tony says, tipping the red tin can. "We'll put in a little whiskey"—he does—"to take the edge off." He caps and shakes it. "The Malloy Special!" he says.

At the sound of his name, Malloy's muscles start twitching. I can tell he'll be on his feet and at the bar in a minute. He sits up, rubs his eyes, and stumbles to his feet.

I wake up Dan, who I know won't want to miss this. Tony pours a big glassful, with real ceremony. "Thanks," Dan says, reaching for the glass. "I could use a drink."

He's got it almost to his lips when Tony yells "No!" and grabs it away from him, splashing some on Dan's jacket.

"What kind of rotgut *is* that?" Dan says. "It smells like kero . . . "

"That's a drink for Mr. Malloy," I say, my voice real steady.

"Mr. Malloy," Tony says, the soul of good cheer. "A little refreshment after your nap?"

"How very thaw'ful," Malloy says. "You gemmun are too kin'." He picks it up for a toast. "You won' be joining me?"

Me and Tony and Francis all say *nooooo* like we never touch the stuff, but Dan, who's still woozy, says, "I'll have one."

"Oh, no, Daniel," Tony says, real fatherly. "You know how the missus feels about strong drink on the breath." Dan looks at Tony like he's flipped his wig, grabs the bottle of Malloy Special, and pours himself a drink.

I stand there stunned, but Francis thinks fast and says, "I'll have one too," and lunges down the bar, knocking over the bottle and throwing Dan's drink to the floor.

"You moron," Dan yells. "Look what you done."

"No harm," I say. "I'll clean it right up. Mr. Malloy, you go right ahead without us." Dan starts making like a bloodhound, screwing up his face and sniffing.

"Don't mind if I do, gemmun," Malloy says. "To your health."

Let me tell you, Francis, me, and Tony hung on every drop. But the old souse just throws it back, smacks his lips, and says, "*That's* the tonic."

"Another, Mr. Malloy?" I say, at the ready.

"I'd be most obliged," he says. Behind the bar I'm pouring straight from the can. "Bottoms up!" I says, placing the glass down before Malloy.

"That *is* kerosene," Dan says, finally putting two and two together. Malloy tosses back the second drink and his eyes cross; his face turns a pale green, and he sits back on his stool like he's looking for something to lean against. Then he says, "Absolooly delishus," and smacks his lips.

"Give Mr. Malloy another," Dan says, in the spirit of things.

"Yes, another," Francis says. I'm already pouring. This time Malloy's face goes white and his lips pull back from his yellow teeth; he flashes open his eyes and they seem red as fire, like the kerosene has lit something deep within. He stands up and sways and holds his stomach and says, "I'mmm jus' . . . a wee bit . . . dizzy."

"I'm sorry to hear that, Mr. Malloy," I says. "Maybe a brisk walk in the evening air will help."

"Do you know how cold it is out there?" Francis says, then recollects himself. "Cold enough to get the blood circulating again," he says.

"Yes," Tony says, like a doctor of medicine. "A walk in the evening air might be just the thing."

Malloy tried to speak but couldn't; his tongue flapped around a bit but just strangled noises come out. Dan buttons his coat, puts on his gloves, and takes an arm. Tony hurries around and gets the other. Francis and me get into our coats and joins them.

We didn't walk far with Malloy—it was too damn cold, and the wind was howling like a soul in torment— just far enough from Maroni's to find a nice big snow-drift. We'd unbuttoned Malloy's shirt and the top of his pants to give him full benefit of the evening air, and we laid him down gentle on his back. It was snowing so thick, he soon had a clean white frosting.

"Hardly seems right, leaving him here like this," old mournful Francis says.

"You're right," I say and start shoveling snow on Malloy's bloated belly.

"What are you doing?" Francis says.

"What does it look like I'm doing?" I says.

"Joe's right," Dan says. "It would be a sin not to make the end come as quickly as possible." He and Tony join in, and pretty soon Malloy looks like a drift himself. Francis stands back and quotes from the Bard of Avon or someone, "Sweet is death that puts an end to pain."

"Let's get out of here," Tony says, "before *we* freeze to death."

Five hours later we were back at Maroni's, each thinking what it was we done, and hoping we'd get the money soon. But we were worried. The radio said it was fourteen below, the worst storm of the year, with twenty-one inches of snow expected.

"They might not find him till spring," I said morosely. "It's going to be a long winter."

"We can't wait that long," Francis said. "Maybe we should dig him up."

"Can't risk it," Dan said. "We might be seen."

"What do we got to be afraid of?" Tony said. "He's just a homeless bum. We give him a couple drinks and he walks out of here and has no place to go."

"But we gave him a couple drinks of kerosene," Dan says, "and I'm the beneficiary." He's afraid, it's clear, but suddenly all I can see is him skipping off with the loot. I look at Tony and Francis and see them thinking too.

"Maybe we should all move in together for a while," I says.

"Considering your admiration for the Florida sun," Tony says.

"And your well-known love of train travel," Francis says.

"We'll keep it in my safe," Tony says.

"No way," I say. Because I don't trust him neither.

"I'll hold it," Francis says. "Where is it?" He moves toward Dan, who shoves him away.

"Keep your hands off it," Tony says. Pretty soon we're on the floor, all four of us, rolling around and yelling and kicking and biting and punching when the door opens and a wicked cold wind sweeps a flurry of snow across the floor. It's three in the A.M. and we all look up, surprised.

"Iss a col', col' night out there, my frens," Malloy says. He stands in the doorway covered with snow, like a ghost. "I'm col' right down to the marrow in my bones." He crashes up to the bar and grabs it tight with his hands. "A bit of the ol' liquid magic to warm me up?"

I'm a little ashamed about what happened after that. We tried antifreeze straight, and with a turpentine chaser. We gave him gin and tonic with a twist of lye. We made Crêpes Suzette with white gas. We fed him sardine sandwiches laced with carpet tacks, and lean corned beef with a special mustard of rat poison. Each of these treats set him back a bit; his eyes would roll in his head, he'd stagger and sway and crumple in a rotten heap on the floor. We'd crowd around real solicitous and take his pulse, but even when we couldn't find one—and here we'd whoop and holler and grab each other and dance—Malloy would just grunt and roll over and scratch his arse.

The worst was when Dan McLaren went a little crazy and tried to chop up Malloy with an axe. I caught it in mid-swing, probably the bravest thing I ever did. "Stop it," I said. "Count to ten." He was growling in his throat like a mad dog. "You're his beneficiary, for Christ's sake," I said. "You can't *murder* him."

"He's got to die," Dan said. "He's got to die."

"He'll die," Tony said, real soothing. "Don't worry; he's going to die."

Finally we decided that drastic measures were called for. We took a cab down 149th Street to the Harlem River. It was the second week in February, four in the morning, and every sane soul in the city was safe and warm in bed. We'd given Malloy a generous glass of disinfectant and he was dead on his feet. With all those rocks in his pockets and those lead ankle warmers, he was a heavy bastard and we pretty much had to drag him.

We struggled to the center of the bridge and stood there looking down. Ice floes jammed the river, which hardly flowed beneath us. As you can imagine we were in a hurry because it was three below zero and we were involved in a serious crime. The struts and supports of the bridge were black with grime, and only the faintest glints of light came off the ice. "It looks deep enough here," Tony says, and we all stop short.

"Let's do it fast and get it over with," Francis says.

"Okay," I says. "Everybody ready? On three. One . . . two . . . " We pulled back and heaved-ho on *three*, but somehow Dan slipped on the ice and we got all unbalanced. Malloy's leg hit one of the girders and he bounced back and we all fell down except Dan, who almost went over the side; he caught on at the last minute with his hands and he hung there pathetically, screaming for help. I nudged Malloy toward the edge while Tony pulled Dan up and out of harm's way. Just then Malloy's eyes opened and he says, real soft, "Where am I?"

"Jesus Christ," I says to Francis. "You bring the frying pan? Listen, bang the bum over the head, will you?"

So Francis starts swinging, making a racket, bashing around in the dark. Now Dan's up and with us, but whimpering like a little baby. He and Tony and I grab Malloy under the armpits and heave him up. Francis is banging away; there's blood on Malloy's forehead, I can see it even in this little light.

"Stop it," I hiss. "Help us throw him." So Francis drops the frying pan and grabs Malloy's feet and his

shoes come off and just as Malloy's body slips away
from us for the last time I see his feet, all horny and ugly
and black as hooves from the frostbite. We stand there
in the dark, breathing heavy. It takes a long time, but
finally we hear the splash, far away, not as big as you
think a body would make.

Then, wouldn't you know it, Francis breaks down
and starts wailing, "I'm a murderer. I'm a murderer."

"Shut up, you little nance," I said, "or we'll toss you
over. Let's go," I said to the others.

That's when we saw the cop. He'd been standing
there watching us, God knows how long. "It was his
idea," Francis screamed, pointing at Tony. We all ran
like hell, but I was the only one that got away.

I went back to my room, of course, and cleaned out
of there in minutes, with the bucks I'd managed to save.
I got across to Harlem and then downtown to Grand
Central Station and I took the first train out of the city
to Philly, where I holed up in a real fleabag for a day or
two and read the New York papers.

Francis and Tony and Dan were arraigned for first
degree murder, and I was a wanted man. The three of
them told everything—my picture was front page.

I got my hair cut short, like a convict, and I pasted on
a mustache. I wore a hat and fake glasses. Oh, the
papers were full of it. How we'd killed this poor innocent bum in cold blood, how we'd planned it all. MUR-
DER SYNDICATE the headlines said. They didn't know
the half of it. Malloy? Innocent? Besides, they never
found the body, just as well for those guys, what with
the frying pan and carpet tacks and antifreeze and turpentine.

I made it to Chicago and I changed my name. I got a job tending bar at a place called O'Farrow's on the south side, rough but I couldn't be picky. I kept up with the trial as best I could. In August the State of New York fried my old friends, all three, on the testimony of the cop. The fact that Dan had the policy in his pocket when they were arrested didn't help much.

So it's December again, see, about a year since it all happened. Things were no better in Chicago than they'd been in New York, and Mr. O'Farrow is moaning and groaning worse than old Tony ever did. "I'm not worth a plugged nickel," he says. "No one's got money for drink, though drink's what they crave."

I want to tell him to pipe down, he's getting on my nerves, but he's the boss. I'm busy wiping glasses, and I say, "Just give it time, Mr. O'Farrow. The joint'll jump, you'll see."

The door opens and this guy in a Salvation Army suit comes in; he'd been in before, and he gave me the willies. "Go away," I say. "You're scaring off business."

"A nickel in my palm," he says, "assures a nickel's less sorrow for the unfortunates of this world." I didn't say nothing. "It assures," he says, his voice rising, "a nickel's less of Satan's own distillation to distort the judgment of good men like you."

"Go away," I says. "You got the wrong guy."

He shakes his head, real sorrowful, and turns to leave. But another man comes in just then, all bundled up, a swirl of snow surrounding him. He sits down at the bar and takes off his hat and he says, "Ah, kin' sir, would you credit a bit a that liquid magic to a poor old man not long for this worl'?"

There was red fire in his eyes, hellfire I tell you; there was a scar on his forehead. I'd know that face anywhere, you bet I would. I'll be damned if it wasn't the devil himself, Michael Clancy Malloy.

HELL TOUPEE
by Steven Bauer

Based on the Universal Television series *Amazing Stories*
Created by Steven Spielberg
Adapted from the episode "Hell Toupee"
Written by Gail Parent and Kevin Parent

*There are a whole bunch of stories in the hairless city;
this is one of them.*

HARRY BALLENTINE GRASPED THE FAKE LEATHER
handle of his attaché case in a steady hand as he followed the prison guard past the cells on Murderer's
Row. Though his three piece pinstripe suit came from
J. C. Penney's, not Brooks Brothers, though his watch
was a Swatch, not a Cartier, though his tie was not silk
but polyester, he was up-and-coming, and his wardrobe
and accoutrements would soon follow.

He walked with the square-shouldered determination
young Clark Kent would have had if he'd decided to be
an attorney-at-law rather than a newspaperman. Behind
his somewhat bookish glasses, Harry's eyes were wide
with his belief in truth, in justice, and in the fact that
both could be ferreted out from the welter of lies and in-
equality which give modern life its peculiarly piquant
texture.

He'd been first in the hearts of his parents, first in his
undergraduate class at Clarity College, first in his class

197

at Probity Law School, and was now last in line—the gofer—in the firm of Brack & Worth, Attorneys-at-Law. He was only twenty-three years old; his bar scores weren't even back yet.

The guard opened the cell door, let Harry in, and locked it behind him. For a moment Harry's heart fluttered—only for a moment—because the man he confronted, though he seemed harmless enough, with his jowly self-pitying expression, his shiny bald pate and watery brown eyes, had put bullets into the heads of three lawyers.

"Who are you?" the man, Murray Bernstein, asked suspiciously. It appeared he'd been outfitted in mattress ticking. Harry opened his attaché case and sat down, handing Bernstein a business card.

"Harry Ballentine of Brack & Worth," he said. "Sorry my name's penciled in."

"But I called Worth," Bernstein protested. "Last year I made out this simple little will, and I got Worth. Now when I really need help, they send me somebody not even out of his teens."

A bit affronted, Harry sat back and adjusted his glasses; he knew he looked young, well-scrubbed, like a diligent Senior Patrol Leader, but he had his pride. "With all due respect, Mr. Bernstein, since you admitted to killing three lawyers on three separate occasions, Mr. Worth thought it would behoove him to send someone the firm wouldn't mind losing."

Murray shook his bald head. "Oy," he muttered.

"Not that I'm not enthused," Harry reassured him. "This is a *fascinating* first case to have."

"Oy again," Murray said.

"So, now it's the time for you, the accused, to tell me

what you think is everything regarding the circumstances surrounding the alleged incident or, in this case,
incidents, which you, the accused, have been accused of
vis-à-vis the crime.''

"What?'' Bernstein asked, his eyes narrowing. "I
may have had to kill the other three lawyers, but at least
I understood them.''

"Tell me in your own words what happened.''

"That's the whole problem,'' Bernstein said in
wonder. "I don't remember. One day everything was
fine; the kids were fighting, the wife made me mad. Life
was great. We were a nice, close family.'' He pulled his
wallet out of his pocket and showed Harry a snapshot.
"This was taken a week ago.''

Obviously they'd shoved themselves into one of those
four-for-a-buck booths you find at K marts; Mrs. Bernstein's hair had been bleached, and she wore dangly earrings. The kids—a boy and a girl—clearly had chosen
Dennis the Menace as their hero. Bernstein looked like
Bernstein, except he had a full head of brown beauti-
fully cut and perfectly combed hair.

"Did you say a week ago?'' Harry asked.

"Yeah,'' Bernstein said. "Well, a week and a day.
We had it took the afternoon I got the hairpiece. See?
Everybody's happy, no one's killing anyone. I look ten
years younger.''

"And then?''

"And then I don't know. The whole week's a big
yellow blur. I went to sleep an accountant and woke up
the Zodiac killer. I don't *know*. I was always a very
quiet guy; the wildest thing I ever did was put guppies in
the principal's gas tank.''

"You know something, Mr. Bernstein?'' Harry

Ballentine said, rising. "I believe you. And I'm going to defend you to the best of my ability. I'm going to work day and night for you, even after my mother says, 'Harry, turn out the lights, you're killing your father.' "

"What number *oy* we up to?" Murray Bernstein asked.

"Three," Harry said. "Why?"

Because he didn't drink coffee or smoke cigarettes (he was a lawyer, after all, not a private investigator), he had to take diet pills to stay awake. Ms. Beth Hollander, his assistant, had littered his immaculate desk with the styrofoam pillows designed to keep fast foods hot. But he was having none; he'd never felt less hungry. So engrossed was he in the case of Mr. Bernstein that he noticed only the words issuing from Ms. Hollander's unusually sensual lips—not the lips themselves, not the way she crossed and recrossed her shapely legs nor the smooth swish of her nylons, not the way she looked at him, as though no diet pill in the world could curb her hunger. It was three A.M. She was getting tired of being sultry.

Harry stood and paced. "Read back what Murray's wife said."

Beth Hollander sighed. "First she confirms her husband was a wimp," she said, looking at Harry as though she were speaking of him, "and then, I quote, 'Murray was a good boy until he got that hairpiece from Hair & Now. Then he changed."

"Go on."

" 'He stayed home from work the next morning, wouldn't get away from the mirror. He kept admiring how handsome he looked. He whispered to me in French—he hadn't done that since we were in college. The sex was great. That's when I knew for sure something was wrong.' "

"Was he on medication?" Harry wondered, scratching his head. "Could it have been alien radio waves directing him through his fillings? Does he have an identical twin? Was he having trouble with his digestion? There's got to be something." He shook his head and paced. Then he glanced at his watch. "Ms. Hollander, you should go home," he said, not unkindly, looking at her at last.

"Mr. Ballentine," she said. "Harry." It was time to throw caution to the winds; hell, it was almost time for breakfast. She paused, put down the affidavit from which she'd been reading, and wriggled on the couch; she rose, placed a hand on her right hip, raised her chin, and pouted. "Here we are, the only ones in the whole building. We've spent almost an entire night together. Do you ever think of me as a woman?"

"Ms. Hollander," Harry said, his eyes burning with resolution. "I can't think of you as a woman until every criminal behind bars is a woman. I mean until every bar has a woman, until every woman behind bars . . ." He sank into a chair. "I'm exhausted," he said.

"Oh, all right," she said. "Maybe some other time." He watched as she walked past him into the outer office, and stooped to pick up the previous evening's paper the boy had slipped under the firm's door.

She screamed.

Harry rushed to her side and grabbed the paper. TWO MORE BAR-MEN DEAD; KILLER CAUGHT the headline read, right next to a photo of a meek-looking bald man named Floyd King. Perplexed and shocked, Harry turned and stalked back into his office, followed by Ms. Hollander, who was obviously in a state of some excitement. He scanned the article, reading snippets aloud. "Police Chief Martin Hanson quoted as saying, 'If these murders don't stop, there will be hell to pay.' "

Savagely he flung the paper to the floor and walked on it. "Five dead lawyers . . . Floyd King . . . Murray Bernstein . . . hell to pay . . . lawyers . . . bald killers . . ."

He stopped as the clues began to form; in his mind he saw something a little like a dead hedgehog. "Hell Toupee," he shouted. "Get it? A psychopathic hairpiece! Ms. Hollander, what would you say if I told you I was a genius?"

Harry took two more Dexatrim, drank a glass of orange juice, and by nine o'clock had managed to arrange a meeting with his client and Floyd King. He stood staring down at the proof of his theory as both men sat on a bunk, the light from a hanging bulb reflecting off their bald heads.

Leaning in, as he'd seen Perry Mason do so many times before, he said, "Why'd you do it, Floyd?"

"I don't know, Mr. Ballentine," Floyd King said. He was a pathetic, chubby little man with fingers like cocktail franks. "I wouldn't hurt a fly. No, wait a minute, that's not true." Harry's heart was always warmed by a strict regard for truth. "I got me one of those sticky twirly fly strips last summer . . ."

"So what made you take the big jump from catching flies to ventilating lawyers' brains?" Harry asked, in close now. "Just tell me everything that happened."

"I got up," Floyd said. "I ate my puffed wheat. I put on my hair."

"Right," Harry said. "You put on your hair. Tell me about the hair."

It all made sense, Harry thought, on his way to the prison's Possessions Room. Both men had been bald for years and had resigned themselves to their depilation. Both men had been stopped short on the sidewalk in front of Hair & Now by a toupee that had seemed to call out to them. What both had seen was a head of hair so shapely, so perfectly composed, so *real* as to make each of them enter the shop and take out his wallet. Both had undergone a psychotic character transformation after putting it on their heads. Both would go through it again for the feelings of pleasure and power the hairpiece had aroused. This was no ordinary rug.

The guard was getting tired of Harry, he could tell by the way the man dragged his feet and sneered. "My good man," Harry said. "Could we hurry? This is a matter of life and death."

The guard pulled down the box of Floyd King's possessions and gave it to Harry, who checked the contents against the list. "Is that all?" he asked.

"That's all there is," the guard said.

"You sure?"

"Okay, o*kay*," the guard said, pulling a five spot from his pocket. "So I borrowed from the guy. Crucify me."

"It says here there's a toupee in this box," Harry said, showing the man the list.

"You're pulling my wooden leg," the man said.

Harry reached inside a ripped manila envelope and

drew out a single brown hair. "Get me Murray Bernstein's stuff," he said. No toupee. A ripped manila envelope with a single brown hair. Harry held up the two strands and looked at them side by side. He was no expert but he could tell a match like that.

Even as they stood there, the toupee was attempting another thrilling escape. After its incarceration in a manila envelope following the Bernstein massacre, it had managed to rip its way free and slither down the concrete hallways, staying clear of the feet of guards, posing as a large brown fuzzball, as horsehair from an ancient fraying mattress, even as a small meatloaf.

Now it jerked along like an inchworm, heaving its hindpart up, stretching its forepart forward, leaving its natural part untouched. Soon it began to pant in short rodent-like gasps and had to stop to catch its breath; so used to being given rides, the toupee was horribly out of shape. It crouched in a corner, as inconspicuously as possible, avoiding a pair of spit-shined number twelve shoes which hurried past.

In this manner it made its way to the door of the prison. As before, the guard who watched the monitors for any signs of escape was eating, and he didn't see the furball as it scurried across one of the television screens; just beyond that were the bars over which the sign read ABANDON HOPE ALL YE WHO ENTER HERE. Looking right, then left, it gathered courage and slid under the bars. Immediately the prison's alarm system sounded and the toupee's hair stood on end. An electronic voice began repeating, "There is no chance for escape. Give yourself up and you can still have conjugal privileges."

The toupee held very still, and then began to move as quickly as it could, like a berserk dustrag, darting and slithering among the pounding feet the alarm had set in motion. Finally it knew humiliation was its only chance. It found a pair of shoes whose owner was relatively stationary and began to whine and rub itself against the guard's ankle.

The light was poor, the guard distracted by the ruckus. Absentmindedly, he reached down and patted the toupee. "How'd you get in here?" he asked. "Come on, go on. Get." With his shoe he nudged the toupee along, opened a final wooden door that led to the prison yard, and shoved it outside.

Free again, the toupee thought. Heh, heh, heh.

Chief of Police Martin Hanson was having a very good time; he'd once had dreams of being a stand-up comedian, but hardly anyone had ever laughed at him. Still, he tried his best to be a witty fellow. "You expect me to believe that a toupee is responsible for these murders?" he said to Harry Ballentine. "And who was responsible for the St. Valentine's Day Massacre, a padded bra? Charlie Manson's really a girdle in disguise?"

"You'll be sorry," Harry said, "if that hair kills again."

"Sounds like we're headed for trouble. Get it? *Head*ed for trouble," Hanson said, and doubled over in laughter. He looked at Lieutenant Jason Childress, a hang-dog sort of guy, to see if he was laughing. "This is great stuff," he said. "I haven't had so much fun since Jason caught his winkie in his zipper."

Jason wasn't laughing. Neither was Harry.

"I take it, then, you won't help me capture it?" Harry asked.

"No," Hanson said. "But I will help you comb it. You think this is a *permanent* condition?"

"Chief," Harry said.

"Tell you what," Hanson said. "I'll lend you some of my most highly trained men and give them orders to throw out a hair net."

"Go ahead and laugh, Chief," Harry said. "But even as we speak, a killer toupee is stalking the streets of this city."

"This is a hair-raising story, Mr. Ballentine. Hair-rendous."

"He didn't believe me," Harry told Beth Hollander. "Did you have better luck?"

"I talked to the owner of Hair & Now," Ms. Hollander said, "who keeps unusually complete records. The hair is French; it used to belong to a poor woman from Nice who was accused of murder. She was poor and had to sell her hair to pay her lawyer, a con artist who charged 'reasonable rates.' The guy did nothing to help her. The day of her execution, a man confessed."

"You mean she was innocent?" Harry said. "It was the lawyer's fault?"

"This rug's in the vengeance business," Beth Hollander said.

"But *these* lawyers didn't betray her," Harry said. "This isn't France; this is America."

"She left no heirs," Beth Hollander said.

•   •   •

The toupee hunched on the sidewalk outside Hair & Now, waiting for the shop to open. It spied a cheerful, red-cheeked bald man walking up and down in front of the main display window, clearly in the mood to buy. For a moment, it thought of calling out "Monsieur" or otherwise drawing attention to itself, but then realized that any head it wished to ride wouldn't belong to a man who'd wear a rug he found in the gutter. Then it saw the wingtips of Mitchell Crouse, the hirsute manager of Hair & Now. He was whistling and jingling keys in his pocket.

The toupee watched as the prospective customer walked away, clearly wanting to appear nonchalant. Crouse opened the door and the toupee, not losing a moment, slipped through. As it crawled up the counter, knocked a synthetic toupee off the premier styrofoam head in the window, and arranged itself attractively, the bald man entered the store.

Mitchell Crouse was on him in a second. "May I help you?"

"I'm just here to look. Really," the man said.

"There's no obligation to buy," Crouse said unctuously. "In fact, you could even rent, if you wished simply to re-experience the feeling of follicles for a short while. Now why don't you sit down right here and we'll see what we can do for you." The toupee watched as Crouse ran his fingers over the crown of the man's head. "You have a lovely area here for future hair."

The man stood up. "The idea of glue on my head makes me queasy," he said.

"Mr. . . . ahh?" Crouse said.

"Monroe," the man said. "Cliff Monroe."

"Mr. Monroe," Crouse said. "That's what everyone's afraid of at first. But it feels like—like nothing at all, like a second skin. Now let's see if we can't get you looking twenty years younger." He turned toward the window.

The toupee primed itself, lifting slightly off the styrofoam head toward Crouse's fingers. But the louse took a different one, made of MiracleHair, and lowered it like a crown onto Cliff Monroe's pate.

"Fabulous," he cooed. "A perfect fit. This piece seems to have been made for your head. The resemblance to Tyrone Power is frightening."

Monroe grimaced slightly and sank down in the chair. Tentatively, he reached toward the hairpiece, then let his hand fall, "I don't . . . Is it real hair?"

"An exact replica. It's realer than real. Made of the same stuff the tiles on the space shuttle are made of."

"I'd rather have real hair," Monroe said.

"I think I just sold my last . . . No. Wait a minute," Crouse said. He turned back to the window and spied the toupee which now sent waves of Gallic charm in Monroe's direction. "Where did you come from?" he said.

"What?" Monroe said.

"Nothing, nothing at all," Crouse said reassuringly. "I *do* have something in real hair after all. From France. The country of *amour*." He settled the toupee on Cliff Monroe's head, and the toupee went to work.

Imperceptibly it caressed Monroe's scalp, and subtly shifted its contours. Before his own eyes, Cliff Monroe became a handsome man. He sat up, an expression of profound emotion on his face. This time his hands touched his new scalp with reverence. "I don't believe this," he said. "I gotta have this one."

Ah, the toupee thought. Time to dismantle the bar.

Harry Ballentine careened through the streets in his '67 VW beetle; he knew he had no time to waste. If both Bernstein and King had bought the same hairpiece at Hair & Now, then *somehow* the lethal toupee was getting back there. He screeched to a stop beside the store, leapt from the car, and ran in, wild-eyed and breathing heavily. The man behind the counter threw his hands in the air and said, "Don't shoot! There's only twenty dollars in the register."

"I'm after a toupee," Harry said. The man put down his hands and looked with contempt at Harry's scalp. "I can see why," he said. "That one you're wearing . . ."

Harry took out a manila envelope and handed Crouse two strands of hair. "Do these mean anything to you?"

Crouse's face relaxed as he took what Harry offered him. "They *are* very familiar," Crouse said.

"Do you have a toupee made of anything like this?"

"Wait a minute," Crouse said. "Wait just a minute. In fact I just sold . . ."

"Oh, my God," Harry said. "There's no time to waste. You have the owner's name? You do? Good. You track him down, go to his house, his place of work. There's no time to waste. I'll try to figure out the next victim."

"What are you talking about?" Crouse said. "I just sold him the piece. We never do follow-ups. Anyway, I've got a showing to go to this morning. The latest in new fashions for the scalp."

"Listen to me," Harry said. "As long as that toupee stalks our streets, no lawyer is safe. Our entire legal system depends on our apprehending a twisted toupee with a grudge. If it kills again, it'll be on your head."

"Would you like a glass of water?" Crouse asked.

The rug under discussion was on its way to the office of David Zahl, Attorney-at-Law. He was the last lawyer alive in the city who advertised "reasonable rates." After him, the sky was the limit; still, the toupee wouldn't quit until every double-breasted, pinstriped, double-talking barrister in the metropolitan area was dead.

Cliff Monroe, with a handgun in his pocket and murder on his brain, opened the door to Zahl's office. Behind a cheap office-equipment desk, wearing a cheap leisure suit, sat Zahl himself; he was talking to a somewhat overweight middle-aged man.

"Yes," Mr. Zahl was saying. "It's your will. You can leave whatever you want to the world's goldfish."

"You Zahl?" Cliff Monroe asked. "You claim to have reasonable rates?"

"Who are you?" Zahl asked, suddenly edgy. "You with the Better Business Bureau?"

"I'm a killer," Cliff Monroe said.

"Sorry," Zahl said. "I'm not taking any more clients."

"I'll just be going," the man with Zahl said. "I hadn't planned to use my will today."

"Don't move," Monroe said, pulling the handgun from his pocket and waving it between Zahl and the other man. The sound of running footsteps momentarily distracted him; he was even more distracted when the door burst open and a red-faced and panting Harry Ballentine stumbled in. Monroe whirled and pointed the gun at Harry. "Who are you?" he snarled.

"Put that down, mister," Harry said. "I've got no hairs to split with you. I just want . . ." He pointed to Monroe's head, where the hairpiece had slithered backwards, withdrawing.

"How did you find us?" the hairpiece squeaked.

"Simple," Harry said. "I forced myself to think like a French toupee. It's something they taught us in torts class."

"You a lawyer?" Monroe asked, his eyes gleaming.

Harry took a step back. "Not really," he said. "Not at all."

"Okay," Monroe said. "Which one of you wants to die first?"

"I can wait," Zahl said. "Let him go first."

"It's you, then," Monroe said, pointing the gun at Harry.

Harry had to think fast, but he'd done that before. He pointed to a spot on the faded carpet. "Look!" he yelled. When everyone looked, he picked up a lamp and attempted to smash the toupee, but it slipped off before he could squash it. All he got was Cliff Monroe, who promptly fell to the floor.

Later, when he told the story, he'd pause here and regretfully insert his single biggest mistake in the entire case: when he'd burst into Zahl's office, he'd forgotten to close the door. In the melee that followed the lamp, the toupee, in full flight, had slipped out of the office, down the hall, and into an elevator before Harry had gathered his wits about him.

The elevator doors closed on his hand, which he withdrew with a pained yell. Then he watched the numbers ascend until they stopped at Ballroom; he ran up the three flights, now fully winded.

When he pushed open the double doors of the Ballroom, he found himself at a fashion showing of some kind. On a runway, an M.C. stood surrounded by models. One held a surfboard and flexed his pecs; another was dressed as a mercenary and wielded an Uzi machine gun. Next to him stood a playboy in silk pajamas, a tennis player in whites, and a lumberjack, a huge burly fellow with a full beard, a red-and-black plaid jacket, and an axe.

Next to the M.C. was a glittery sign that read "Toupees by Alfred."

"Let's get out there and spread the word," the M.C. was yelling as the models turned around and around, tossing their heads to the left and right. "No matter who your clientele is, Alfred has a hairpiece that's right for you. A hairpiece with style, with flair, with panache, with savoir faire, with suavité."

Harry backed against the wall, his heart pounding. The room was filled with men, some with hair, some without. One with a headful of murder. Among them waiters passed carrying heavy silver trays with lids, setting up a buffet on the far side of the room.

"Bald is passé," the M.C. yelled. "Shape up, America, with an Alfred toupee. You can shower, swim, or skydive in an Alfred. Made of the finest fire-resistant polytrell," he said, whipping the toupee off the lumberjack, "so real, God wishes He'd made it Himself. Here, for example, the Tuf E Nuf, for those who treat their hair rough. Scented with cedar, this baby is so strong it'll pull the QE2 out of drydock. Just try to take it apart, Woody.'' He handed it back to the lumberjack who promptly attempted to rend it with his hands.

Harry Ballentine had to start somewhere, so he reached for the hair of the man closest to him. It came loose easily, and Harry bit it, stomped it, taking no chances; but it wasn't the one he was after. It lay there on the floor pathetically, no life in it at all. Its shocked owner turned as Harry moved on to the next. Unfortunately, this man's hair was growing from his head. When *he* turned, his face was pale with rage and Harry ducked as a fist whipped overhead and collided with a third man's jaw.

The fight spread from there, like ripples from a single thrown rock. Harry found the safest place to be was on the floor as fists flew above him. He crawled around, hoping the violence would jar the wicked hairpiece loose, and it would fall into his waiting and ready hands —he had a penknife, a set of keys, his teeth. ''Help, murder, police,'' the M.C. intoned mechanically over the P.A. system.

Hairpieces flew like scraps of paper in a heavy wind. Harry grabbed one after another, first stabbing, then biting down hard. All he got for his trouble was a mouthful of hair.

Then suddenly he found himself face to shoe with the heavy laces and metal eyes of a pair of brand-new work boots planted squarely before him. He looked up slowly, along two denim-clad legs, to a red-and-black plaid jacket, to a full beard, a weirdly grinning mouth, a pair of glittering eyes, and, perched on top, like a wicked bird's nest . . .

Harry yelled as the lumberjack picked him up and hoisted him high. "A lawyer!" the lumberjack yelled. "Timber!" Harry flailed and kicked, trying to rake the top of the man's head, but his arms weren't as long as the lumberjack's and he kept swiping the air. He felt the man's arms pull back for the throw, and he was lowered just a bit, just enough to grab hold. He whisked the toupee off the huge man's bald head and immediately, bewildered and embarrassed, the man dropped Harry.

But did Harry lose his grip? He fell to the floor with a resounding thud, and he and the toupee rolled over and over, he trying to strangle the hairy little thing, the toupee doing its best to stuff itself into Harry's mouth and choke him to death. They tumbled into the legs of men who fell over them like felled trees. Finally Harry and the toupee had rolled as far as one of the buffet tables; Harry reached up, grabbed a heavy silver warming cover, and slammed it down, trapping the toupee. It battered against the underside of the cover until, exhausted, it finally lay still. "Gotcha," Harry Ballentine whispered. "Call the police."

After the news conference and the personal meeting with the mayor, after the accolades from peers and partners stopped flowing in, Harry took Beth to the jail to see the toupee, now imprisoned in a clear Plexiglas case. They stood looking at it until Harry said, "You know, Ms. Hollander? In a crazy way I feel sorry for anything incarcerated without benefit of representation." Then, finally, he kissed her.

The Chief of Police was there, ready with an apology. "Well, Mr. Ballentine. I guess I should have believed you. You're a good man and you deserve this victory.

He who laughs last, laughs best. Hair-dee hair hair.''

Harry Ballentine said, ''I'll never laugh, Chief, until they find a less embarrassing word for the penal system.''

That ends the story, more or less. Except that later that night, a bald policeman named Officer Schmidt came on guard duty, and the toupee, with its finest French charm . . .

Where there's a wig, there's a way.

NO DAY AT THE BEACH
by Steven Bauer

Based on the Universal Television series *Amazing Stories*

Created by Steven Spielberg

Adapted from the episode ''No Day at the Beach''

Teleplay by Mick Garris

Story by Steven Spielberg

ARNOLD SKAMP LAY IN HIS BUNK, WRITING A LETTER
home. "Dear folks," he began. "I hope you are both
well. We're on our way into action for the first
time . . . "

Below him, the other members of his squad were
playing poker, all except Irish, who sat polishing his
automatic, oblivious to the rocking of the transport
ship, the soft pops of distant mortar fire across the
waters of the Mediterranean. Alone of all of them, Irish
seemed genuinely unconcerned about tomorrow, when
they'd land on the beach at Porto Nuovo to support the
movement of American troops sweeping up the thin
boot of Italy. As for himself, Arnold Skamp was just
about scared to death.

The five who sat around the makeshift card table
were louder than usual, attempting to hide their
uneasiness behind prickly talk and bravado. "I'm with a
great bunch of guys," Arnold Skamp wrote, "and I
know my friends and I will see each other through this."
Like him, they were in their late teens, green recruits,
new to this war business. Ira, the dealer, was a wise-
mouth cardsharp. "Ira and a tall skinny guy we call the

Stick are from New York City and they promised to show me the town when we get home. Ira's going to teach me to be a poker player too." Stick was in fact so skinny his chest looked like extra-wide-wale corduroy.

As tall as Stick, Tiny weighed twice as much; he was from Georgia, a real cracker, and mean. "He's hard as nails on the outside, but a fine Southern gentleman underneath," Arnold wrote. "He thinks I've got the stuff to be a real soldier." Casey, who usually bunked under Arnold and was the kindest of them all, was from Fort Wayne, Indiana. He had a round face and tortoise-shell glasses. "I'd have to say Casey is my best friend," Arnold wrote. "He's real smart and we can just talk about anything. He looks out for me, sort of like the big brother I never had."

And Evergreen was from Los Angeles; he knew all about Sidney Bechet and Fats Waller and Count Basie, people Arnold had never heard of. They all hung together—they called themselves The Club—and though they'd settled on Arnold as scapegoat, Arnold thought if push came to shove they'd stand by him. He longed to really be one of them, and resolved that before the war was over, he would be.

But Arnold Skamp was used to being the outsider. An only child, born premature and subject to croup, he'd been sheltered and pampered, and had grown up a frail bespectacled youngster. His arms and legs had seemed perpetually determined to outgrow and outfox his graceful use of them. He fumbled, stumbled, tripped, and dropped things; he bumped into walls and unsuspecting strangers. He grew to accept awkwardness as his normal condition, to apologize for it, and to take as his due the taunts and jeers of those endowed with

physical grace, comeliness, or self-possession. He en-
vied them, but mostly he admired them, the runt of the
litter who wanted more than anything to be one of the
pack.

It was Thanksgiving, and back home in El Dorado,
Kansas, his parents would be sitting down to dinner
with his aunts and uncles and the cousins who had
ostracized him, and though he was terrified of going
into combat, he was secretly glad to be here, far away
from the farm and the corn and the hogs. He sighed as
the ship rolled and sent the pencil in his white-knuckled
hand skidding toward the margin; he just wished one of
them would ask him to play.

"Okay, gentlemen," Ira was saying, in an exaggerated croupier's voice. "Five card stud's the name of
the game. Devil rides out." He flicked the cards in a circle, and the guys picked them up.

"Well, boys," Tiny said. "Prepare to lose your
drawers. The Lord does provide."

"Jesus, Tiny," Ira said. "Don't give us that cornpone crap."

"What do you mean, *cornpone*?" Tiny said, pushing
back from the table.

"Cool down, soldier," Ira said. "Rule number one
—never let a city boy get you riled in a card game."

"Rule number two," Tiny said. "Don't shovel shit
on a guy twice your size." He settled back, grumbling,
while Ira smiled to save face and pulled out a cigar that
would have made Edward G. Robinson blush. He
peeled off the wrapper and Stick lit it for him with a
Zippo.

"Come on, Ira," Evergreen said. "The stink's bad
enough in here."

"You ain't exactly Private Rosewater," Ira said.

"I'll go up against you in the Mr. Aroma contest any day," Evergreen said.

"Jeez," Casey said. "Can we play some cards?"

In the distance Arnold heard the sound of explosions, louder now; the wind had shifted or the transports were drawing unexpectedly close to land. The others held still, listening too, their banter momentarily forgotten. He looked at them, and then stole a glance at Irish, still silent, still polishing. It was going to be bad in the morning; one of them might get hurt, or even killed.

"So come on," Ira said. "Who's gonna open?"

Stick stared hard at his hand. He pulled out his wallet and as he took out a bill, a snapshot of a teenage girl fell on the table. "I'll open for a buck," he said.

"I'm out," Evergreen said.

"Me too," Ira said, throwing his cards face down. Tiny and Casey tossed theirs in as well.

"You guys can't fold on me," Stick said.

"Looks like we already did," Ira said as he swept up the deck and began to shuffle them.

Tiny picked up the photograph Stick had dropped and said, "Get a look at Stick's peach."

"Gimme that," Stick said, but Tiny was too quick and the picture got handed around as the guys raised their eyebrows and smirked and whistled.

"Did this come with the wallet?" Evergreen said.

"You asshole," Stick said, grabbing the photo away.

Ira had dealt five cards around again, and he picked up his hand. "Deuces, queens, and one-eyed kings wild," he said.

"You can't call wild cards *after* the deal," Casey said.

"I can try," Ira said.

• • •

They played for a while, desultorily, most of them
folding in the face of any possible threat, as if playing
cautious tonight might help them tomorrow. Arnold
watched, then wrote a few lines, then watched some
more. While Ira had the biggest mouth, he seemed the
least apt to bluff. Casey played straightforward poker,
calculating the odds, almost never gambling. Tiny
wasn't too bright, and had the meanest temper. Irish
kept polishing and polishing the automatic.

"Hey, Arnold," Tiny said, concentrating on his
cards. "Gimme a cup of that mud, will ya?" Glad finally to be included, Arnold scrambled down, knocking
into the back of Stick's chair as the ship rolled.

"Sorry," Arnold said.

"Whachit, Arnold," Stick said.

As quickly as he could, Arnold filled a battered tin
cup with coffee, brought it over, and placed it next to
Tiny. He put his hands on the back of Tiny's chair and
peered over his shoulder at two kings and three nines.
"Wow," he said. "Good hand!"

"I'm out," Evergreen said, throwing his cards on the
table. Ira, Stick, and Casey all tossed their cards in too.
"You little snot-nose weevil," Tiny said. "Get away
from me."

Ira had gathered and shuffled the cards again. "Hey,
Arnie," he said. "You know how to play Fifty-Two
Pickup?"

"Come on," Casey said. "Cut it out. It's Thanksgiving."

"He gets on my nerves," Tiny said.

"Leave the guy alone," Irish said. Everyone turned
to look at him. It was the first time he'd spoken since

the card game had begun. His hand moved over the rifle's stock as if enchanted. He shrugged and said, "A clean weapon is an effective weapon."

They got bored with the game after a while and they lay on their bunks in silence, except for Tiny, who whistled until Irish told him to shut the hell up. Arnold stared at the ceiling and tried to imagine the next day. He squeezed his eyes shut to make the pictures clearer, but the only beach he could envision was the rocky shore of Elk City Lake in Kansas, the only deaths he could see were those inflicted on chickens and hogs by his mother and father. He tried to watch himself struggling through the cold blue water, running up the beach as bullets spit sand around him, but not a single picture made it into his head.

At ten-thirty Evergreen said, "Come on, guys. Let's eat. I got the turkey," and they all turned on their sides and watched as he threw a khaki-green can of C-rations on the table. Arnold was caught daydreaming about Kansas and thought at first that a real turkey had materialized. He was further confused when Ira said, "Here's the cranberry sauce," and threw another can of rations on the table.

"Homemade biscuits and sausage gravy," Tiny said.

"Corn on the cob," Stick said.

"Candied yams with little melted marshmallows," Casey said.

Irish threw down two cans and said, "Mincemeat pie *and* pumpkin pie."

Arnold wanted to join in, but wasn't sure how. "I've got the coffee," he said. Everyone looked at him as

though he'd slammed shut the door between them and
their dinner.

"Oh, Jesus, Arnold," Evergreen said. "Why don't
you just fuck off."

It was getting close to midnight, almost time for lights
out. Evergreen was writing in a leather-bound book;
Casey was reading a copy of *Liberty*. Ira played
solitaire.

"Hey, Evergreen," Stick said. "What you writing?
A novel?"

"Only thing he ever wrote was the menu at his dad's
Chili Bowl restaurant," Ira said.

"Least I *can* write," Evergreen said.

"Don't take no brains to write," Ira said, putting the
cards away. "Takes brains to make money. Now who
wants dessert?" He pulled out a plastic bag of chocolate
bars.

"What's the gouge?" Evergreen said.

"You think the price went down? Four bits," Ira
said.

"For a lousy five-cent candy bar?" Evergreen said.

"You don't gotta buy one."

"Hell," Evergreen said. "I'm in."

"I'll take one," Arnold said. He pulled some change
from his pants and it dropped and scattered on the floor
as he tried to hand it over.

"Sorry," Ira said. "All gone." Then he sold a bar to
Casey.

Arnold lay back, feeling bad. He didn't mind being
kidded by them, even felt he deserved it at times, but
when they lied to him or made a joke out of him, he felt

as forlorn as he had in El Dorado when the kids in health class had put flypaper inside the sleeves of his jacket. He just didn't fit in, not in El Dorado, not here; he was beginning to really feel sorry for himself when Casey's hand appeared from the bunk beneath, holding half a candy bar. Just then something exploded not far from the boat and everyone froze, waiting for what would come next. Arnold could hear his own harsh breathing competing with the others when Tiny exploded. He took the candy and held it tight.

"I can't wait to get my hands on those goddamn kraut bastards," Tiny said. "We'll blow them Jerries to hell and back."

"You got it, Tiny," Ira said, but his words sounded tired in the quiet of the bunkroom.

"I'm gonna get me a Nazi too," Arnold said, trying to keep his voice steady.

Stick laughed. "Is that right?" Tiny said. "You gonna get you a Nazi?"

"I am," Arnold said. "I sure am."

"Stop it, Arnold," Casey said. "Let it drop."

Everyone let it drop until Stick's voice, hushed and hesitant, reached Arnold where he lay, holding the taste of chocolate in his mouth. "Ira," Stick almost whispered. "You ever seen . . . you ever seen anyone die?"

"My old man," Ira said. "He had T.B. Used to have these long rattly coughs. One night, me and my kid sister was with the old man, just having some ice cream or something." He paused and took out a cigar. "Anyway, Pop starts on one of his jags, you know, hackin' away. I thought he was choking on the pistachios in the ice cream or something, until I seen the

blood on his chin. So I rushes over to him and I hold
him in my arms and try to get air into his mouth." He
blew smoke toward the ceiling in a long contemplative
stream. "But it was too late. Now every time I think of
the old man I taste this rusty red taste." Arnold peered
down at the two of them. Ira was sitting up, both hands
dangling between his knees as he stared at the floor
amid the drifting smoke. Then Arnold poked his head
over the edge of the bunk and looked down at Casey,
who appeared upside down. "Thanks for the chocolate," he whispered.

Casey was reading, and he glanced at Arnold and
nodded, and then went back to his magazine. When
Arnold refused to go away, he said, "Okay. You're welcome." But Arnold had something he wanted to ask
and he continued to hover until Casey said, "What do
you want, Arnold?"

It was hard to say, but Arnold wanted to admit it at
last. "I . . . I sure wish I could be more like you guys,"
he said.

Casey looked horrified at the confession. "What the
hell is that supposed to mean?" he said.

"Casey," Arnold said. "I'm scared. I'm afraid about
tomorrow. I just wish I could be brave like the rest of
you guys."

"You think we're not afraid?" Casey said softly.
"Can't you see straight? Everybody here's got something to lose. I never seen a bunch of guys more scared
spitless."

This struck Arnold as absurd. "Not you!" he objected. "Not Irish. And for sure not Tiny."

"Tiny probably most of all," Casey said. "He's got
himself a seventeen-year-old wife and a three-week-old

kid. You think he's got anything but them on his mind every minute?'' He reached up and punched the underside of Arnold's bunk. "Go to sleep now," he said. "We'll need you tomorrow."

Ira stood up now and waved his arms as if asking for silence. "All right, gentlemen," he said. "Time for Uncle Ira's Magic Draw. Face cards bring luck. Let's hear it for face cards all around. Who wants to be dealt some luck?" He limbered his fingers as if preparing to pick a lock, and then shuffled his deck, a master sharp. He pulled the first one off the top and showed the queen of hearts around. "All *right*," he said. "Lucky face for me. Who else wants some luck?"

He tossed a card at Stick. "Lucky face," Stick yelled, showing the jack of diamonds.

"Me too," Evergreen said. "Jack of spades."

"Got it!" Casey whooped, showing the king of clubs.

"King of spades!" Tiny said. "Lucky face like mine." Irish smiled and showed the jack of hearts.

"What about me?" Arnold said.

"Aw," Tiny said slyly. "Did we forget old Arnie?" He strode over to Arnold's bunk and yelled, "Flying lessons," and in seconds he'd been joined by Ira, Stick, and Evergreen, each of whom took an edge of Arnold's blanket and lifted him off the bed. The four of them tossed him into the air. His arms flailed as he left the blanket and hung for a sickening moment in limbo; then he fell and hit the harsh wool trampoline and looked up into four maniacal, yelling faces. The room tilted and he was flung into the air again. The door burst open and they dropped him rudely; he and the blanket both hit the floor.

"Knock off that racket," their sergeant said. "You

girls got a big day on the beach tomorrow and I want
you bright-eyed and bushy-tailed. Now lights out." He
flicked off the switch and slammed the door.

In the darkness, Arnold grabbed his blanket and
climbed back into his bunk, ashamed, as though he'd
been the cause of the melee rather than the victim. He
lay there as the ship rolled, resolved to show them all
tomorrow: he'd be brave. He'd get himself a Nazi. By
tomorrow night, they'd have accepted him without
reservation—no more jokes, no more laughingstock.
He'd be a hero tomorrow. He'd show them.

At dawn they attacked. Thousands of men left the
transport ships and boarded the LSTs. As they prepared
for the assault, the warships in the Tyrrhenian Sea bom-
barded the coast with artillery, trying to soften the
Italian beach, to beat back the Germans enough to give
the troops a purchase. The gray sky was streaked with
fire.

"Away all boats!" the command horn blared, and
the LSTs, loaded with frightened, determined men
began to cross the last stretch of sea to the coast. The
Club huddled, shivering, as they moved through the
chop. Arnold felt dismal, cold, terrified; his resolve of
the night before seemed empty words to him. He looked
at the others and wondered how they felt. A man named
Granville stood at the helm; he'd been through this
before and he seemed like the model of calm. "Chins
up, guys," he yelled above the din. "We're almost
there!"

"Come on, Chief," Tiny said. "Pour it on."

Granville turned around and stared at Tiny. "Cool it,
soldier. You'll get your chance to win the war." He

looked at their sergeant and said, "Looks like you got yourself one tough bunch of palookas." The sarge shrugged, lit a cigarette, and tossed the burnt match into the roiling sea.

Before Arnold was even sure he knew what was happening, he heard a high whine; the sergeant yelled, "Down!" and a huge plume of water shot up alongside the transport as the air exploded and the ship was knocked rudely sideways in the chop. Arnold screamed and fell on his face in the deck's mud and water. All the others scrambled low, muttering and cursing. Granville laughed, and the sergeant took a long pull on his cigarette.

"Can you spare a butt?" Granville asked the sarge. "There ya go, hot shots. Welcome to World War Two."

They all stood again, staring at the fast-approaching shore. The waves of men before them were already scrambling off the LSTs, struggling through the remaining water as little bullet spurts shot up around them. Arnold could see soldiers running forward across the beach; some stopped short, staggered backwards as though they'd hit an impenetrable field, and fell. He felt someone beside him; it was Casey, who handed him his lucky face card.

"It's all yours, glory boys," Granville yelled. "Go get 'em."

The first round of bullets hit around them, a flurry of high whines followed by small waterspouts. "Lock and load!" the sergeant yelled. "Lock and load!" The LST came as near the shore as it ever would, and the men vaulted off the deck and into the hip-high water.

Arnold's first sensation was of the water's coldness

and thickness; he churned forward as if through sand, holding his rifle before him. Around him the water was alive with the stinging spray of artillery fire and he felt a sudden sharp pain in his chest, three quick punches as if he'd been stabbed by an icepick. He grunted in surprise and pushed against the pain. His body stopped running; from somewhere a message had been sent for his legs to cease their movement, and he began to topple forward, as if some joker had tied his shoelaces together.

And then he felt a lightness he'd never experienced before. He was suffused with radiance, as though his heart had begun spreading silver through his veins. In his jacket pocket, the king of clubs shone like the sun burning through fog, and for the first time in his life he knew the descent of grace. He took breathless pleasure in how his body felt, as he moved in perfect synchrony with the waves, the sand, the fire of artillery and mortar. He was impervious in his new strength, his new perfected musculature, his airy, floating purposefulness.

The water had lost its stiffness; it ebbed away to his ankles, and then he was on the beach. Beside him, Casey ran, his face white with fear; the other members of The Club floundered around him. Arnold looked in wonder at their ungainly dodging, their terrified faces, as the bullets thudded around them, spraying their legs with sand. He felt no fear at all, and he knew he was safe. Before him, bodies of men he didn't know fell to their knees as if in prayer; he charged through smoke and fire, avoiding the bullets, the explosions, the carnage, as if he ran through a downpour without a drop of water touching him.

"Hit the dirt!" the sergeant yelled. "Belly-walk it!" The members of The Club began hauling themselves forward on their elbows and knees, all except Arnold who kept running, effortlessly, without tiring. Before him the scene spread out and he saw with preternatural clarity what needed to be done. On a hill overlooking the beach, the Germans had built a shelter, a pillbox with a rectangular slit from which machine-gun and automatic rifle fire rained down upon the heads of the Americans. Someone had to destroy the stronghold if any of them were to survive the assault, and though it looked impregnable, Arnold knew he'd be able to get there.

The Club reached a gully; German fire from the pillbox stitched the sand inches above their heads. The sergeant grabbed the radio from Irish and tried to reach one of the American warships, calling for backup artillery. But the radio was dead. As Arnold stood on the lip of the gully looking down at them, he felt great love and great pity. It was clear they didn't understand— they needn't be afraid, and they needn't call for backup. He'd be fine.

"Come in, Command," the sarge yelled. "We are penned in at base of pillbox. Require immediate artillery backup." There was no response. "Okay, boys. Let's see what we can do. Rifles at the ready!" He stood up, wiped the air with his arm, and screamed, "Gung ho!" He leapt to the edge of the gully and immediately machine-gun fire ripped through him; he toppled backwards and lay face up as blood stained his jacket.

"Oh, God," Stick screamed. "They got the sarge. Oh, my God."

"Knock it off!" Ira yelled. "Just stay low. We'll figure what to do." An explosion nearby showered them all with dirt and flak. Dazed and slightly crazy,

Evergreen propped the sergeant's body into a sitting position. "It's okay, Sarge," he said.

Didn't they understand? Arnold thought. Didn't they know that all they had to do was lie low and wait for him? He wanted to speak to them, to reassure, but he knew they wouldn't hear. With his rifle at the ready and the grenade pack secured around his shoulder, he began his ascent of the hill.

He heard his name yelled as he ran; he heard the awe and tension in their voices. Around him the bullets careened and whined; but he was swift as wind, and he felt cool and protected, as though air moved among his bones. He darted and dodged, climbing, climbing, until he was under the overhang of the pillbox, right below the dark slit from which the fire issued.

He pulled off the grenade pack, yanked the pin, and calmly counted to eight. Below he could hear his name being sung, being chanted. At the last possible moment, he stood and thrust the grenade pack into the mouth of the pillbox and dove away, down the hill.

But before it exploded, one of the Germans tossed it back out. And then, as if he had all the time in the world, Arnold ran to where the grenade pack lay, picked it up, and, in an effortless overhand, a move of supreme grace, tossed the grenade back into the slit.

When the pillbox exploded, Arnold stood and watched as the burning planks, the screaming enemy soldiers, the sandbags, and radio equipment flew into the air. Below him, far below him, as though he had the vantage point of a hawk, the members of The Club were standing and cheering. Now they cleared the lip of the gully; now they surged forward, their rifles spraying, freed of their fear. Although he knew they couldn't see him now, through the thick smoke, he motioned them to follow; although they couldn't hear him, he called them all by name. And then he faded into the air, his natural element, where flight in all its perfect power and grace was his.

Though Granville had taken a bullet in the shoulder, he'd managed to pull the boy's body ashore after the first wave of enemy fire had killed him. There were three neat holes in the boy's chest, as though his rib cage had been punctured with an icepick. Poor kid, Granville thought. Probably hadn't even known what hit him. The poor kid hadn't even made it to the beach, had landed face down in the surf over Porto Nuovo. Granville had stayed low until someone, somehow, had gotten the pillbox, and the fighting had moved further inland, and the exploded beach was calm again.

He went through the soldier's pockets, to put his effects in a small bag. He found a playing card and what seemed like a letter home. *Dear folks,* the letter began. *I hope you are both well. We're on our way into action for the first time, and I'm scared to death. But I'm with a great bunch of guys, and I know my friends and I will see each other through this. I know you'll like them as much as I do. They're good men and better soldiers than I could ever hope to be.*

Granville looked up to see the mud-streaked faces of the men he'd brought ashore that morning. "Hey," one of them yelled. "You see the hero? You see that goddamn little guy?"

He didn't know who they meant; he shook his head. In his right hand he held the dead soldier's letter; in his left hand he held the king of clubs.